DOWN THE RABBIT HOLE

CYNTHIA TERELST

In memory of Shorty
Thank you to the beautiful girl, with a kind heart, who
rescued him

KEEP IN TOUCH

To be notified of future releases, and to keep up to date with other news, please join my newsletter.

https://www.subscribepage.com/p9p9yo

CHAPTER ONE

Emily

WELCOME TO ALMA.

I smiled to myself. The smile was a lie, just like the sign. I hadn't stepped foot in this town for seven years. I wasn't welcome back then and I wouldn't be welcome now.

The main street was just the same as it had been for the past twenty-five years. Broad, with car parks on either side of the road, and a garden down the middle. Wide verandahs on the shopfronts stretched all the way to the roadway—a blessing when unpredictable Queensland storms rolled through. The signs on the awnings were faded, some unreadable. It didn't matter. If you were a local, you knew what the shops were. If you weren't a local, you'd just be driving through, anyway.

I ignored my memories as I drove past the shops and the people strolling down the footpath. It was hard enough driving through town but seeing someone I knew would be worse. I wasn't ready.

I sighed. I'd better get ready. The first stop I'd be making was the rural supplies, the Phillips' Rural Supplies. My stomach tightened thinking about them. All I needed to do was pay off Dad's account. I didn't need to engage in conversation. Get in. Get out. That was the plan.

The gravel crunched under the ute's tyres as I pulled into the car park. Clutching the steering wheel, I forced my breath to steady. The huge shed loomed overhead like a monster ready to crush me. But it was the monsters inside I was more worried about. Resigned, I reached out to turn the car off and got out.

Without looking anywhere except the counter, I walked through the big roller door and past pallets of feed, seed, and fertiliser. Grit ground under my feet. I don't even know why I was so worked up. I'd left this town seven years ago, gone to university and started a successful business. I was happy. I was happy just being me, and they couldn't take that away from me. I squared my shoulders.

When the blond-haired guy at the counter turned to me, I nearly faltered. Nearly. I made certain my steps didn't slow.

Recognition spread across Corey Philipps' face. He opened his mouth and I expected him to say *Lemony Emily,* the charming nickname they'd given me as a child because they thought I was sour. Putting up with their shit, year after year, it was no wonder. Before he could utter a word, his mother appeared beside him. Her long blonde hair was tied back in a ponytail so tight it had to give her a headache. She put a hand on his arm as if in warning before looking me up and down.

"Hello, Emily. It's so nice to see you."

I doubted it. She'd never been happy to see me before.

"Hi, Mrs. Phillips. I'm here to pay off our account."

She considered me, a moment too long. The beginning of a smile lifted the corner of her lips like she knew a secret she was eager to divulge.

"It's over $3,000."

She didn't even need to check the computer. How many times had they discussed my father's account amongst themselves? Worse yet, with others? The debt wouldn't be worse than any other farmers in town. Dad would have paid off the previous year's debt after harvest, then would have needed seed and fertiliser among other things for the next planting. All farmers had a revolving account. That's just the way it worked. Except the prospect of Dad's account being paid was almost non-existent compared to those other farmers.

I maintained eye contact with her. "That's fine."

Her eyes widened.

I pulled out my card. "Do you have an exact amount so I can pay it now? I'll need an itemised invoice, please."

She hit the computer keys with attitude and flourish, printed an invoice and handed it to me. I glanced at the total and handed her my card. I wasn't going to scrutinise the invoice in front of them. Mrs Phillips examined the card like it would reveal more than just the numbers on its face. Her eyes lifted to mine; eyebrows raised as if in challenge.

"Credit?" Her voice was smarmy, presumptuous. She inserted the card into the machine, her finger moving toward the credit button.

"Savings, please."

Her finger paused for a moment. "Oh, of course."

What was that in her voice? Disbelief? Disappointment

that she couldn't say Jim Watson's daughter paid off his credit account with credit of her own?

I flexed my fingers. I'd nearly made it through my first encounter. I hadn't embarrassed myself. I'd actually been quite composed. Corey had moved away, which helped with my tenseness.

Mrs Phillips handed the card to me with my receipt.

"Thank you," I said, taking the card from her.

As I turned away, Mrs Phillips said in her saccharine voice, "I'll be out to visit your dad soon."

Please don't.

I strode away, passing my nemesis on the way.

"See ya, Lemony."

Stiffening, I picked up pace, not relaxing until I reached the safety of my car. My hands shook when I considered where to visit next. I'd reward myself with the servo last. There were new owners there. At least they would have no animosity towards me.

By the time I made it to the servo, I was worn out. It had been hard to control my nerves as I entered each establishment and each time, I'd chastised myself. I was an adult now. I'd left this town and its people behind. I was strong then and stronger now. Those people should no longer have any effect on how I felt.

I shook my hands and dispelled any nerves before pulling the servo's glass door open. The shop was the complete opposite to what I remembered. The lino beneath my feet was whole with no gaping holes or cracks. The shelves were clean and well-stocked. The lights above shone bright without a single flicker. My nostrils were not filled with mustiness. I turned to the counter and was greeted by a smiling face. It was the first genuine smile I'd seen all day. The lady's long teal top was patterned in vibrant pink and orange, bringing out the golden hues in her brown skin.

"Hi. I'm Emily Watson. I'd like to pay off our family account please."

"Jim's daughter?" Her accent was strong, maybe Pakistani.

I stared at her, surprised she recognised my name so readily. "Yes."

"It is my pleasure to meet you. I'm Aisha Sharif."

I was taken aback by her friendliness and familiarity. How did someone who only moved to town two years ago know my name?

"Thank you. It's nice to meet you, too."

She nodded, still smiling.

"I'd like to pay off our account please."

"There is no account here."

That didn't make sense. Dad always had fuel delivered to the farm, and if he needed parts for machinery, he'd likely buy it from the servo. The look on my face must have reflected my thoughts.

"We wiped that account months ago when we learnt of Jim's illness."

"That's OK. I'm happy to pay."

"No. No. There is no account to pay."

I considered her. People who'd known my dad since he was a child held onto his account, most likely discussing his failure to pay. Yet, these people who'd been here for two years, had wiped it.

"Your father, he welcomed us, me and my husband, to town. Helped us to settle in. Invited us into his home. Him and the Bairds were the only ones."

Dad may have been a hard arse. Strict. Cold, at times—well, most of the time with me—but he had a kind heart. The fact that Luke's family were the only other family to welcome the Sharifs didn't surprise me.

Luke had been my best friend for twenty-five years. The only person who'd made life here bearable. He was the person I looked forward to seeing the most on my return. Just thinking about him brought a smile to my face. His easy grin. His messy hair. His warmth. Him.

The door opened behind me. I shivered as the cool breeze caressed the back of my neck. The clack of heels against the lino made my stomach drop. I turned as the footsteps approached the counter. My whole body froze at the sight of Bianca Phillips striding towards me. I was amazed my autonomic nervous system continued to function.

Bianca flipped her blonde hair over her shoulder, her hips swaying. Stopping in front of me, she stretched up to her full height, pushed her chest out and cocked her hip. She had always liked reminding me that she was taller than me, always looking down on me. She scrutinised me and scowled. "Emmaline. Mum said you were in town. I didn't believe it."

Emmaline. No one but Bianca Phillips had called me that since the accident. The day I'd reopened my eyes I was known as Emily. Everyone respected that, except Bianca.

OUR THIRD-GRADE TEACHER stood at the front of the classroom, smiling at me. "Welcome back to class, Emily. We've missed you."

I shifted in my seat as everyone in the classroom turned to stare at me. It wasn't the first time they'd stared that day.

They'd stared on the bus when Bianca had made sure they'd known of my presence by whispering and pointing. They'd stared as I'd entered the school, my arrival announced like wind crossing fields with no wind breaks. Stares and whispers everywhere I turned.

"Her name is Emmaline," Bianca pointed out, contempt filling her voice.

My heart raced. My hands escaped to under the desk, and I clutched at the hem of my skirt. Luke, who was sitting beside me, spoke for me. "We call her Emily now."

"She can't just change her name," Bianca said, her voice rising.

She turned her body to face us, full of attitude, sneering. What fucking eight-year-old sneers at another? I shrunk away from her. Luke sat up straighter.

"Bianca, people shorten their names all the time. If Emily wants to be known as Emily, that's what we'll do." The tone in our teacher's voice indicated it was the end of the discussion. I sat there, my heartbeat thumping in my ears. Luke's warmth at my back reassuring. He didn't waver. Neither did Bianca.

"I don't know why she gets special treatment just because her mum is dead."

JUST LIKE THAT DAY, I shrunk away from her. Words evaded me. Bianca smiled, knowing exactly what effect using my full name would have.

Mrs Sharif cleared her throat. "Is it just the petrol you'd like today, Bianca?"

Bianca's face hardened as she rolled her eyes and turned to Mrs Sharif. "Yes."

"That will be sixteen dollars please."

Sixteen dollars. She didn't need fuel at all. It was just an excuse to come in here to see me. Bianca pulled her card out and tapped it against the machine. As she walked towards the door she said, "See you around, Emmaline. I'll let Luke know you're home."

As soon as the doors closed behind her my stomach unclenched. I was nauseous. Trust Bianca to take me back to being an insecure child. I should have called after her that Luke already knew I was home. That she knew nothing about Luke and me. That we were still best friends even after seven years apart. That Luke was not, in any way, interested in her.

But I didn't.

"You shouldn't give her so much power over you," Mrs Sharif said, her voice gentle.

"I know. I didn't mean to."

"Do not worry. Sometimes strength comes little by little. You can grow, but a person like Bianca is stunted."

I pressed my trembling hands against my thighs and took a deep, calming breath. "Yes, you're right. Thank you."

"You go now. Go to your father. Dalir and I will visit soon." She reached across the counter and squeezed my hand.

Mrs Sharif's kindness gave me a serenity I hadn't felt all day. As I drove towards the farm, I tried to hold onto that serenity. Field after field passed by. Their rows of leafy green vegetables orderly, nothing out of place. This kind of constant could bring harmony to one's soul. I didn't feel it. The peacefulness I'd felt minutes ago eroded kilometre by kilometre. When I turned into the driveway and spotted the house, the serenity disappeared altogether.

CHAPTER TWO

Luke

"THE PHILLIPS LOOK like they're doing another facelift," Jim noted as we drove past the rural supplies. The signage was getting a new paint job, like it did every year or so, even though it was a huge job and the paint work they had was perfectly fine. They even went pink once to humour Bianca.

"Mrs Phillips must be bored again," I said.

"I guess that means she'll get some remodelling, too." He laughed. He wasn't wrong. She and Bianca would often go away for a girl's weekend to Brisbane and come back new and improved—new clothes, new lips, new boobs, whatever took their fancy.

I laughed with him. They were such fakes, and right then, so was I. My laughter faltered. There was something I'd left unsaid. Something I'd withheld from him for two weeks. I took in a deep breath. This was it. I needed to tell him. We were nearly back in town and my time was running out. I tapped my fingers against the steering wheel, willing the words to come. "Emily's coming home."

Jim stiffened and faced me. "What?"

"Mum called her a couple of weeks ago to tell her you're sick."

"I don't want her here."

This is exactly the reaction I expected. I kept my voice even. "You don't have any choice. She'll be here today."

"I don't need her here. I just want to die in peace."

I let out a harsh breath. His knee jerk reaction wasn't good enough and I took it upon myself to tell him so. "Don't be an idiot. This is your chance."

The wall of silence was erected so fast, like how tectonic plates moved during an earthquake. Jim turned away, his composure becoming rock hard.

In response, the lightness bouncing through my body at seeing Emily crashed to a halt, like when an excited dog bounces around and then he's ordered to sit.

I pulled into the servo, got out of the car, and stretched. It had been a long morning. Mum and I rotated taking Jim to his cancer treatment appointments. This fortnight was my turn. When I'd started taking him, our one-hour drive to Toowoomba had been spent mostly in silence. But each month I'd learnt more and more about the man who was Emily's father. I'd come to understand him, and his actions over the past seventeen years.

I rolled my shoulders as I put the nuzzle in the tank and squeezed. Peeking at the side mirror, I watched Jim close his eyes and rest his head against the glass. His treatment always exhausted him. Hopefully, it was also exhausting his tension.

He didn't want Emily back here and I knew why, but we couldn't go back to the way things had been. It was time to make things right.

As I walked into the servo, Aisha's smile greeted me. Her long dark hair was tied loosely at her neck.

"I met your Emily today."

My heart rate quickened. "She's here?"

"Oh yes, and she's more beautiful than you said. She came in here to pay off Jim's account."

I laughed, feeling light for the first time all day. She was more than beautiful.

"Everyone in town is talking about her."

I sighed. It was inevitable. As long as they didn't start with their normal crap, there wouldn't be a problem.

"Bianca found her here." Aisha's smile disappeared. "She said one word and your girl froze."

I stiffened. "What word?"

"She called her Emmaline."

I gripped the counter, willing the anger bubbling in my veins to dissipate. I'd hoped after all these years that the town had moved on. That Bianca had moved on, but she was still as much a bitch as ever, living up to her name: Queen B. Why hadn't Emily waited for me to come into town with her? I sighed. I understood why. She was strong and independent. She'd made her way in the world and she wasn't going to let them take that away from her, but the power of negative memories could take their toll.

This stupidity had all started because Bianca had asked to give a presentation about her time as *Miss Alma*. It was scheduled for the day after Emily's accident, seventeen years ago.

She came to school wearing her crown, all excited and ready to glow in the attention she would receive. Because the school was reeling with the news about what had happened to Emily, her presentation never went ahead. She'd held a grudge since that moment and did everything within her power, and her family's power, to turn everyone against Emily.

"How is Jim?" Aisha asked, bringing me out of my thoughts. I straightened up and ran a hand through my hair.

"Tired. It was his last treatment today." I glanced at the man in the car. He knew his days were numbered and just like everything else in his life, he accepted it with no fuss. Aisha held out the machine to me and I tapped my card.

"Well, then, best you get him home to Emily."

I nodded and headed back out to the car. We'd found out two weeks ago there was nothing more the doctors could do for him. Mum had contacted the children from oldest to youngest. Emily's two older brothers and her older sister couldn't, or wouldn't, come home to help him. Only Emily was willing to put everything aside to return—to return to a home and a man who were not full of warmth.

"Aisha said that Emily has arrived," I said as I got back into the car.

Jim opened his eyes and sat up straight. "She was in town?"

"The word is that she's been around paying off all the accounts."

"No one asked her to do that," he said, his voice hard.

"Do you think she would want to owe those people anything?"

He grunted. I knew he wouldn't want to owe them anything either, but circumstances gave him no choice. Most of his medical treatment had been covered by the health care system, but because he had a less common form of cancer, a lot of his medication was not covered. They'd cost thousands of dollars.

I didn't want to argue with him about it. Over the past six months I'd watched him decline. He had been his same stubborn self to start with, not wanting our help. But as the cancer spread like the fog that drifted across our farms on a cold morning, his resistance had declined. And as his resistance declined, I learnt about the man who I'd once thought was an arsehole.

"I don't want her to go into debt just to save face."

"I'm sure she hasn't. Her business is doing well."

He nodded, then turned his attention to the fields we drove past. They were nearly ready to harvest. Jim's jaw clenched as we approached his farm. His hands, once strong, now pale and wrinkled, clutched his skinny legs.

I pulled into the driveway and parked next to Emily's ute. I knew it was Emily's because it was newer than anything around here and her business logo, *Land Reinvigorated,* was on the tailgate. The car was bright blue, her favourite colour. I smiled; only Emily would choose something other than the traditional white for a business car.

I was going to see her any moment and my body reacted in every way possible. Anticipation bounced around my chest. I wiped my sweaty palms on my shorts and then pushed them against the steering wheel, trying to steady them. Once satisfied I was as composed as I could be I hopped out and got Jim's wheelchair out of the boot. Before I got to his door, he'd opened it and stepped out. He waved the wheelchair away.

"I don't need that."

Stubborn old man.

"Right." I left the wheelchair near the back door and stood to his side. "Do you want me to help you to the house?"

He peered at the stairs and then moved his eyes back to where we stood. Letting out a sigh, he nodded. I took hold of his arm and started toward the house. Something caught his attention in the field and his feet stilled. I followed his line of sight. Energy buzzed through my body. Emily was crouching, studying the ground. She appeared small amidst all the space. Reaching down, she pulled out a weed and examined it.

"What the hell is she doing?" he said.

She was doing what every farmer does. She was checking the condition of the soil. As she stood up, her tanned legs unfurling, she shook the dirt from the weed's roots and turned it in her hands. We stood and watched as she slowly turned around and looked at the empty fields surrounding her. When she turned in our direction, she stopped. Even from where we stood, I could see the concentration on her face—the frown and stony expression. Jim and I stared at Emily, and she at us, across the expanse.

Silence surrounded us. There wasn't even a breeze to rustle the leaves of the poinciana beside the house.

"Take me inside," he said. I stood still watching Emily.

Emily tossed the weed and came towards us. My heart rate picked up pace the closer she got. Thump, Thump. Thump, Thump, Thump. I took all of her in—her athletic build with curves in all the right places, her short brown hair that still made me smile to this day, and her round face.

Jim shifted beside me. "Now."

It was too late. She was too close. I saw in her green eyes

the moment she registered her father's condition. Her eyes widened and her mouth went slack. An instant later her face became neutral. A well-practiced façade. I still had hold of Jim's arm. We stood close, but totally separate, like cherries on the same stem.

CHAPTER THREE

Emily

"Hɪ, Dᴀᴅ." I tried to keep my voice calm even though I found it hard to breathe. My father was nothing like the man I'd left seven years ago. His face was slack and wrinkled, as if all the fat and tissue had disappeared, leaving nothing but skin. His clothes hung off him like they were two sizes too big. His hair, once thick and rich brown, was now thinned and dull.

I didn't want to stare, so I turned my attention to Luke. He was the complete opposite to my father—young, tanned, fresh. His naturally messy blond hair glinted in the sunlight. We video called regularly but it was nothing like seeing him in the flesh. My stomach lifted like when Luke and I were driving fast on a backroad and we hit the crest of a hill.

"Hi, Emily." Luke's voice was deep, warming me from the inside. His presence calmed me, as it always had. I wanted him to hug me like he always had. I wanted to feel his strength and steal a little. The selfish me just wanted him. But I couldn't have him. Ever. He belonged here, with his family, on their family farm, and I belonged anywhere but here.

"I need to lie down," Dad said gruffly.

He made to move off but teetered. Luke and I reached for him at the same time. His arm was no longer strong and muscular beneath my fingers. When I was little, before the accident, he would lift me above his head and spin me around. I doubted he would even be able to carry my bags in the state he was in. Dad stared at my hand on his arm and pulled his arm away. I ignored the tears that sprung into my eyes. He'd never wanted me here before, so I don't know why I thought he'd want me here now.

Well, I wanted to be here, and he'd just have to live with that.

Luke said something to him as they walked away. I couldn't hear what it was, but the tone was harsh. Dad turned his face away from Luke like an insolent child. I'd never heard someone speak to Dad like that. Even as our family had fallen apart, and resentment had torn at the edges, no one had used that tone with my father.

I grabbed my bags out of the car. As I followed them, I turned my attention to the house. Taking in a deep breath I considered how its general state reflected that of my father. It had never been anything glamorous, but it had always been kept neat. The light blue paint on the weatherboards was peeling and the windows were covered in dust from the empty fields. It probably hadn't been painted since I'd left. We'd painted it every five years—my brothers, sister, and me. It was like the passing of the baton as each one left and the next oldest was left in charge. The last time I'd painted it, it was my last year at home. There was no one left to help me, except Luke. He was always there. For me.

I watched as Dad and Luke climbed the four steps up to the verandah—Luke holding Dad steady, matching his slow steps. Luke's muscular legs tensed and relaxed. How many times had I stared at those legs at football training as he practised tackling? They looked as good today as they did back then, even if his calves, quads, and glutes were less defined. Taking a breath in, I moved my attention away from Luke's legs. Dad and Luke stopped at the top for Dad to have a rest. I didn't know he was that sick. I hadn't known he was sick at all until the phone call from Luke's mum. It was two weeks ago.

Two weeks ago, when I'd learnt that my father had six months left to live.

I'D LOOKED at my phone and saw Luke's home number. I'd smiled to myself as I'd answered and swung my chair away from my computer. I'd rather talk to Luke than do work any day.

"Hi, Luke."

"Hello, Emily dear."

I sucked in my breath, surprised it wasn't Luke. Was he OK?

"Hi, Bernie."

She must have heard the concern in my voice because she spoke quickly. "Luke's OK."

I sighed.

"I do have some bad news though. Your dad is not well."

I sat up straight. "Not well?"

"No. He has cancer. He's been getting treatment for the

past few months. The doctors have told us there is nothing more they can do."

"What does that mean?" I needed to hear her say it. I stood up and went to the window. I stared out but didn't take anything in.

"The treatment hasn't reduced the tumour and the cancer has spread. He has one treatment left. The doctor said because it was experimental, they need to go through the whole course of treatment. Otherwise, they'd have stopped by now.' She sighed, a light feathery sigh, like the prickling spreading across my skin. "After that, they'll just be managing his comfort and pain."

"How long?"

"Six months at most."

Six months. I rested my hand against the window as dizziness took hold of me. There was no point asking questions. He was dying, that's the only thing I needed to know. I nodded to myself. "I'll need to contact the others."

What was the best way to do that? My mind ticked over, messaging through social media was probably my only option. I almost forgot I was in mid conversation with Bernie until she spoke. "I've contacted your brothers and sister. They're not coming home."

Of course, they weren't. For my last five years at home, I'd been alone with my dad. They'd called on special occasions but that was it. I'd never seen them. Even my sister, who was closest in age, never made an attempt to include me in her new life. Sometimes I wondered if it was just me who was excluded or if none of them spoke to each other. Our family had broken in more ways than one after the accident.

"I need to finish off a couple of jobs and then I'll come

*home." It wasn't really home, not anymore, but I didn't know
what else to call it.*

*"I'm sorry, Emily. Steve and I will be here if you need
anything."*

I MADE my way to the stairs, catching up to Luke and Dad
quickly. It hadn't dawned on me until later that they'd known
he was unwell for months and had never told me. I didn't have
time to be angry with them, not then or now. I needed to help
my father. I needed to do something about the empty fields
and increasing weeds, all while remaining involved in my
business, remotely.

I followed them into the kitchen and watched as Luke
walked Dad to his room. I put my bags down on the faded
vinyl floor. Their mumbled voices reached me where I waited.
Luke's voice was no longer harsh. I turned my attention to the
kitchen, old but functional. The cupboard faces were all pine.
The bureau against the wall held all the good china, Mum's
family china. We used it on birthdays and other special days. I
would always feel excited when we did. It was like we were
having a meal with Mum. I could see her sitting next to Dad
smiling at him and him smiling back.

Pine and eucalyptus filled my nostrils, indicating the
room had recently been cleaned. I ran my fingers across the
table. The varnish had worn off years ago. Roughness from
the woodgrain brushed against my fingers. I walked to the
fridge and yanked the door open. It was empty except for
some milk and a casserole dish. I pulled the dish towards me
and peered through the glass lid. Cottage pie. My mouth
watered.

"From Mum," Luke said as he came into the kitchen.

"I thought so. Did she clean as well?"

"She didn't want you to have to worry about it."

I nodded. Bernie was always thoughtful. Every year on my birthday she would deliver us this very meal. Luke would eat with us. Even as the numbers at the table dwindled as my siblings left home, it felt like we were a family. I closed the fridge door.

"What am I going to do, Luke? There's so much work." My shoulders slumped at the weight of what I was facing. Luke covered the distance between us and wrapped me in his arms. I sank into his chest; his warmth and strength embraced me. I breathed in the freshness of trees and earth. The softness of his cotton shirt caressed my cheek. It felt good here. So good. Safe.

"Spending time with your dad is what's most important." His warm breath brushed my hair as he spoke. I nodded.

"How do I spend time with someone who doesn't even want me here? It's like nothing's changed."

Luke gave me a squeeze before he pulled away. "Let's go for a walk."

As we made our way down the stairs, I took hold of the handrail. It wobbled under my touch. Another thing to fix, especially for Dad, who needed it to be secure and safe in his condition. At least the treads were still solid. Except the bottom one which was cracking and being held up by bricks.

Without even saying where we were going, we took the path to the river. It wasn't really a path anymore, more like a track, a narrow line of compacted dirt. Dad hadn't planted this year and weeds had started to invade the empty fields surrounding us. I'd need to start with that. It would get worse in no time.

"Your dad will come around," Luke said, interrupting my thoughts.

"You reckon?"

"I know he will. He knew you were coming back, and he didn't tell you to stay away."

I glanced at him. I guess he had a point. He smiled at me. I trusted that smile. It had never let me down before, but I didn't expect much from my father. He wasn't a horrible father. He didn't hit me or yell at me or neglect me. He was just emotionally vacant most of the time.

I stopped on the track and glanced around. "And this, what am I supposed to do with this?"

"It's too late to plant a crop."

"I can't just leave it as it is. Those weeds will invade the whole farm soon. Then they'll move onto your farm."

We kept walking until we reached the tree line along the river. I examined the seven Eucalyptus torquate trees Dad had planted when I was a child. Though not native to the area, they had grown tall and strong. I loved the drooping grey-green leaves; they were the epitome of the eucalyptus. The best thing about the trees were the coral pink flowers that burst from their buds in spring and summer. The clusters of flowers reminded me of the fireworks we sometimes watched at the football ground on New Year's Eve.

Luke had installed a possum nesting box in one of the trees to encourage native wildlife back. He said because the trees weren't old enough to have formed natural hollows in the trunks, possums had nowhere to nest. He had not only put nesting boxes on our farms but throughout the whole district, much to the disgust of our local farmers. They thought possums were pests. But Luke thought it was a privilege to be close to such unique wildlife and he knew living in harmony with them was not impossible.

"Are the mum and her twins still in the box?" I asked.

"Yes." He took his phone out of his pocket. After some tapping, he gave it to me. On the screen were the mum and her babies, sleeping snugly in the box. "She's been in this box for three years now."

I handed the phone back, smiling. Installing the cameras had been his idea. He said it was easier than climbing a ladder and checking the box himself. It was also less invasive, which I'm sure the possums appreciated. He'd also installed bird boxes around the farm. He learnt quickly that he needed to install some sort of guard on the boxes to prevent the possums from raiding them. Who would have thought that possums would drag birds out of their boxes and kill them?

I walked on, towards the river. When I took in the sight in front of me, I stopped in my tracks. The water was barely flowing. It was a murky, shallow mess. Run off and erosion from the farms bordering the river had changed the natural flow and the silt had built up on the banks. Luke and I had swum here as children. There hadn't been much water then, but the coolness of the water and the shade created by the trees, had made it feel like paradise. This was no paradise.

What had happened here?

CHAPTER FOUR

Luke

EMILY SUCKED HER BREATH IN. Her sadness hit me as she turned to face me. "This is bad, Luke."

"I know. The farmers think access to water is their right and they'll use every last drop of their allocation because they can." I clenched my jaw. It was hard to live among such ignorance. There was no use talking to them. They wouldn't listen, even if Emily showed them how much things could be improved if they farmed sustainably. "The cotton farmers upriver have improved their practices. They use much less water than they once did, but the amount is still huge."

She nodded. I didn't need to tell her. She was the one who'd taught me everything I knew about the environment and farming sustainably. And that's exactly what she did in her business, teach and help others while giving her best to the environment. Her father and my family had changed our crop five years ago to one requiring less water and fewer chemical inputs based on her teaching, unbeknown to her.

She huffed. "And then it's the insecticides and pesticides they use. It all has an effect on our environment." She glanced between me and the river. "Rivers are dying, salinity has increased, fish stocks have declined by ninety percent, but these people don't care because they have water on tap."

She shook her head and turned away from the river. When we reached the edge of the field she stood and stared out at it. "I don't have the time or energy to change farming practices in this area. My business helps farmers who want help, not those who have their head stuck in the sand."

"They won't listen. I've tried. They'll listen to you even less."

She nodded. We both knew it was true. History was proof.

WE SAT at the back of the farmers co-op meeting with our parents. A representative was there from a prominent fertiliser company talking about a new product that helped retain moisture in soil when used at the tilling stage. The more he talked, the more fourteen-year-old Emily became agitated. She shifted in her seat beside me, wringing her hands together. As soon as the man paused, Emily jumped up. Her dad reached out to stop her, but her words were already coming.

"If we didn't till the soil, then the soil would be protected. It would mean it would be better for crop production. We wouldn't need your magic product."

Everyone in the room turned and stared at Emily. I studied them all. Not one of them were friendly. A lot of them gave her a mocking smile. Some scowled. Others rolled their eyes.

Mr Phillips piped up. "Control your child, Jim."

Emily turned to her father. He sat, passive. She took that as permission to continue and turned back to the rep who was considering her.

"If you don't till, what do you propose will happen with the crop residue?"

"Nothing—"

Mr Phillips spoke again. This time directly to Emily. "Sit down. We don't need to hear your rubbish, little girl."

I was ready to jump up and tell Mr Phillips where to shove his little girl statement. Emily may have been young, but she was the smartest person in the room. Mum held onto my arm. Jim squared his shoulders and sat up taller. He rested his hand on Emily's side and turned to Mr Phillips, opening his mouth to speak.

The rep spoke up first. "I'd like to hear what the young lady has to say."

Emily ignored every person in the room, except the rep. "Leaving the crop residue would help with reducing weeds and would reduce evaporation. It will also help water infiltration."

I smiled at Emily. Her use of technical terms and her confidence in delivering them didn't surprise me. Learning this stuff was her passion. If she got money for her birthday or Christmas, she would buy books about sustainability or subscribe to science publications. She read articles on the internet. She would often talk about what she learned when she came over for dinner.

"And how would you get nutrients into the soil?"

"I would plant cover crops and I would rotate the crops."

"You would need new machinery to plant crops without tilling," the rep said. He, too, was ignoring everyone else in the room.

"Yes, but it reduces soil erosion, which then reduces costs in the long run through less inputs. So, the machinery pays for itself in the end. And it decreases run off. Our rivers will be cleaner."

One of the farmers interjected. "We're farmers, girl. We don't have money for new machinery."

And then another farmer. "And who cares about the river, as long as we have enough water to use?"

And another. "Who wants to waste money on cover crops?"

I swear, it was like we were back in the dark ages. Why didn't these people listen? Statements flew around the room, getting louder, until the rep's voice boomed out, "OK. Let's get back to it." When he turned to Emily, his voice was less intense, "Thank you, young lady, for sharing your views. You have given us a lot to think about." He gave Emily a smile. "OK, then, Mr Phillips will be stocking this product..."

As he continued to talk, Jim and my parents ushered us out of the meeting.

"WHAT ARE YOU GOING TO DO?" I asked Emily. She always had a plan.

"I'm going to plant a cover crop to help with the weeds. It will get some nutrients back into the soil, too."

I nodded.

"You knew that already," she said nudging me. "What cover crop have you been planting?"

I smiled. She was the expert here; she knew cover crops like the back of her hand, but she didn't show off about it. This was the Emily I remembered.

"Your dad and our farm plant French White Millet."

Both farms had implemented cover crops after fourteen-year-old Emily's speech. It was the one sustainability method Jim had implemented before Emily had left home. A way to show the rest of the town that he supported her.

"It's probably the best option. Sixty to ninety days of growth is ideal, so it doesn't take extra moisture from the soil," she said.

"Yes. We don't let it grow longer than that."

"The student is learning to use the force," she said, smiling and hip bumping me.

"Obi Wan taught me well. What else are you going to do while you're here?" I asked as we headed back to the house.

"I'll work in my business and look after Dad at the same time. I'll stay for as long as Dad is here."

My stomach dropped. I always knew she wasn't going to stay, and I would never expect her to, but knowing I'd have to let her go again was hard. Just having her back made me feel like life was the way it was meant to be. But her happiness was more important than mine, and she'd never be happy here.

As we neared the house, we saw a person approaching the back steps. Mrs Phillips.

CHAPTER FIVE

Emily

"WHAT DOES SHE WANT?" I sped up. I didn't want her disturbing Dad. When she reached the stairs, I called out, "Can I help you?"

Mrs Phillips whipped around. When she spotted Luke and I, her eyebrows raised. She covered up her surprise by plastering a smile on her face.

"Emily dear, I just came by to see how your father is."

I gave her an identical smile. "He's resting at the moment. I'll let him know you dropped by."

"Resting...oh yes, OK."

I stopped myself from rolling my eyes and saying 'yeah, resting, you know the thing people do when they're sick'. She looked to the screen door as if my father was going to appear and invite her in. I moved to the stairs to block her in case she decided to make herself at home. Her sickly floral perfume made my stomach turn.

"I'll let him know you came by."

She nodded. "If you need anything, Emily, just drop into the store. We're happy to help."

Happy to stick your nose into our business, more like it.

"Thank you, Mrs Phillips."

Luke joined me at the bottom of the stairs. I hoped it would encourage her to move on. She made as if to leave and my breathing calmed. Until she turned to Luke.

"Luke darling, you should come to dinner again soon. Bianca would love to see you."

I stiffened. Luke went to dinner at the Phillips'? And Bianca would love to see him? Fucking Bianca could go die in a hole for all I cared. She'd been trying to get her claws into Luke for as long as I could remember. Had she succeeded?

"I'm very busy at the moment."

She patted his arm, smiling coyly. "You're always welcome."

Funny how I wasn't welcome.

I watched as she turned away and ambled back to her car. Not just any car, the latest model Land Cruiser in burgundy. She'd probably chosen that colour to highlight her blonde hair, the same golden colour as Bianca's. Bianca had always tried to make me feel inferior by referring to my brown hair as plain. Mrs Phillips didn't hide the fact that she was checking out the place as she went. I detested that family. I didn't move from my spot until she reached her car. I gave her a snarky wave.

"I'm going to buy a chain and padlock tomorrow."

Luke laughed. "Yeah, otherwise they'll all be dropping in to check on you."

The dinner with Luke and Queen B was itching at me. Luke and I shared everything, even after seven years apart but him going to dinner wasn't something he'd mentioned. I guess he didn't have to tell me everything about his life. I just always thought he had.

"Is this dinner thing a common occurrence?"

He sighed. "I went once. Queen B tricked me into it."

"Tricked you?"

He sat down on the stairs. I joined him but couldn't look at him. I didn't want him to see the hurt on my face. How did dumb as dogshit Bianca trick one of the smartest people I knew?

"Remember when the farmers co-op had that bachelor auction for drought-stricken farmers?"

How could I forget? It had been a fun idea. Each bachelor was auctioned off and the winner would go on a date with their bachelor. The thought of Luke standing up on stage, uncomfortable with being in the spotlight, shifting from foot to foot had made me laugh.

"And Bianca won my auction."

No need to remind me.

"You didn't speak to me for a week when you found out."

I gave him a small smile. Poor Luke. It wasn't even his fault.

"Well, she started talking about dinner with her family and I thought that was it, that was the date."

"But it wasn't."

"No. I turned up to dinner to find out it was just a precursor for the date she'd planned the next day."

"And you didn't tell me this."

"I was scared you wouldn't speak to me for a month if you found out."

Knowing Bianca was close to Luke and I wasn't, was like

torture. What right did I have to be upset about who he went to dinner with, though? We were friends. Best friends. That was it.

Even if I wanted more. He didn't. So, friends were all we could be.

I couldn't be angry with him for something that was out of his control. Even if he should have known better. Bianca was always up to something. He'd never mentioned her again after that and I figured she'd just lost interest in him. I assumed that all those years at school, she'd only found him attractive and worth pursuing because she thought I wanted him and when I'd left, the fun of liking him disappeared with me.

"How was your dinner? Did Queen B cook for you?" I grinned at him.

"Hell no. I wouldn't be here to tell the tale if she did."

I laughed. "Remember the time she made meatloaf for the district show and the judges couldn't eat more than one bite?"

"Exactly. Her cooking invites death."

We bumped shoulders. My chest was light. My limbs were light. My heart was light.

My breath caught when I looked into Luke's eyes. My heart beat fast and loud at the intensity I found there. I needed to look away, needed to do something so I didn't get lost in him. Without command my hand reached out, my fingers found themselves in his messy hair, pushing it away from his face. My hand drifted down, away. I should have pulled it back to me, but it was still attracted to him, like how groundwater always found its way to the fissures in rocks. I touched his chest, fingers light against his warmth. Luke's lips parted. Those lips...

The fly screen door squeaked open behind us. What was I

doing touching Luke? I pushed against his chest and laughed. But it was too late to be attached to our conversation. Blushing, I diverted my eyes.

Dad stepped out. He was steadier and less pale. Shuffling to the chair on the porch he considered us both. How many times had he given us that what-are-you-two-up-to-look over the years?

I jumped up. "Would you like a cup of tea?" I asked Dad.

"That would be good."

"Luke?"

"No, I need to leave in a minute."

That would mean I'd be left alone with Dad. My stomach sunk. We hadn't been alone for seven years. I didn't know what to expect. Certainly not an outpouring of love but I hoped it wouldn't be flat out silence. My hand shook as I opened the kitchen door, leaving them alone on the porch.

CHAPTER SIX

Luke

I SAT in the chair next to Jim.

"How long is she staying?" he asked, looking out upon the land.

"As long as needed."

"You mean until I die." The frankness of his statement stilled me. That was exactly what I'd meant but saying it out loud just felt wrong.

"Yes, until then."

"And after that you're just going to let her go?"

"She has a life to go to. A life away from here."

He grunted. "Sometimes you have to fight for what you want."

"I can't expect her to stay."

He turned to me. His hard stare had me looking down at my feet. A heavy ball formed in my stomach.

"Nothing's changed." His voice was as hard as his stare.

"Being with the one you love should outweigh everything else."

It didn't matter. Stay or go, her love for me was different to what I felt for her. Friends were all we were meant to be.

But what did matter was them and their relationship. He needed to make an effort, to change. "Like you can talk."

"Old habits are hard to break."

"You call pushing your daughter away a habit?" I matched his hard stare. Seven years ago, I would never have spoken to him like this. Seven years ago, I wouldn't even have had this conversation with him.

"This isn't the place for her."

"You're not making sense. You want me to ask her to stay, but in the next breath you say she shouldn't."

"Stay doesn't have to mean stay here—"

"That's the last of the milk," Emily said, walking out with a cup of tea for her dad. "Nothing left in the fridge, no long-life in the cupboard, no powdered milk."

"I haven't been shopping for a while," Jim said, taking the cup from Emily.

"I'll grab some stuff tomorrow while I'm in town. After I buy a chain and padlock for the gate."

"Buy what?"

"Mrs Phillips dropped by earlier. Wanted to see how you were apparently."

Jim grumbled, "Couldn't give a shit about me for the last few months but you turn up and she cares all of a sudden. Bloody busy body."

"The whole CWA will be turning up next," Emily said.

Jim nodded and took a sip of his tea.

"I'm going to grab some millet seed, too."

"What for?"

"To get rid of those weeds."

"What does it matter?"

My shoulders stiffened at the edge in his voice. At first, I thought he was angry with Emily and I was ready to step in. When he shrugged, I realised it wasn't Emily who'd upset him, more likely his mortality. I guess you could lay alone night after night, staring at the ceiling, knowing you're going to die and come to terms with it on some level. It didn't mean you couldn't be angry about it sometimes.

Emily gave him a steady stare. "I can't in good conscience leave this farm covered in weeds. Can you imagine how many chemicals they'd use to remove them?"

"What else can't you do in good conscience?" Jim said.

I was ready for Emily to say leave you here to die alone. But her staying here to be with Jim had nothing to do with her conscience. It had to do with love. I knew that type of love.

I HUGGED Emily before she went up to the stage to collect her award. She was smiling broadly as she accepted the trophy from the Head of Science at the University of Queensland. She shook his hand and stood there for photos. I clapped loudly with Jim and my parents. I was proud of her. She'd worked so hard over the past few months competing against other high school students in the state.

She went to walk off stage, like the other recipients before her, but the Head took hold of her elbow. He was handed a microphone.

"We have been astounded with Emily and her submission.

The detail and accuracy were beyond what we were expecting. The University of Queensland, along with additional sponsors, have decided to award Emily with a full paid scholarship for a degree in Sustainable Farming."

Emily stood open mouthed. I turned to Jim who smiled and applauded loudly.

I knew that Emily would be leaving me, but this made it all too real. Maybe I held some tiny little bit of hope that she'd stay but this moment showed me how stupid that hope was. How was I going to live my life without her? Where would my daily dose of happiness come from?

But I did not share those thoughts with her. They were my own selfish thoughts. When she returned to her seat, I hugged her.

"This is the best day ever," I told her. "You are going to uni."

My heart broke, but I would never show it.

INSTEAD OF SAYING anything about her dad's impending death, she said, "In good conscience I couldn't sell the farm with the full water allocation."

"You won't be. I've been reducing the water entitlement as the farm has become more water efficient."

Emily's head whipped around. "What?"

"Each year I've been making improvements, changes around the place."

"Since when?"

This was it. This was Jim extending an olive branch. How far would he go? Would he tell her that he'd been putting plans in place since her speech when she was fourteen? That he'd hid those plans from her? That he'd waited until she'd left before implementing them, because he didn't want to tempt her to stay?

"Since you left."

He raised the cup to his lips ending further conversation.

CHAPTER SEVEN

Emily

I WATCHED Luke's car drive away. I watched it all the way to his house in the distance. It was lucky our grandparents were so close growing up that when they bought neighbouring farms, they built the houses relatively close together. It meant Luke and I didn't have to go far to see each other as we were growing up.

The silence from Dad had me on tenterhooks. I unclenched my hands and then wiped the sweat off on my shorts.

What do you say to someone you barely knew? Start with small talk? It sounded ridiculous but I couldn't think of a better way to start.

"The river is pretty low," I said.

"Yeah, it keeps dropping."

I waited for more. Would he say more? This was so awkward.

"Some farmers upstream have dug huge dams and diverted water into them."

"Diverted water?" That was illegal. Dams were permitted to be built with the understanding that they were to be filled naturally from surface water and run off. Farmers were not allowed to take water from the river to fill their dams and they were only allowed to store the amount of water noted on their licence. If these dams were huge, how much water had they taken from the river? I was scared he meant the farmers had built dams the size of those on cotton farms upstream. The cotton farm dams looked like they were the size of a town. Knowing water allocations in the area, dams that size would store more than allowed.

"Well, they say the dams filled naturally. I suspect they're doing something dodgy."

Silence hung between us as I waited for him to continue. He sipped his tea and looked out beyond the railing. Should I ask him what exactly he meant by dodgy? If I did, would he just dismiss me like he did when I was a kid? I couldn't stay silent. How would things be different if we didn't change the way we did things? "What do you mean?"

"Well, think about Jonesy's dam across the road...it's not always full. It depends on the season and irrigation."

I shifted in my seat to look at him and then looked across the road towards Jonesy's dam. It was true, it fluctuated depending on whether it was the start or end of the growing season and rainfall.

"From what I've seen when I've driven past those other farms, their dams are always full, even when they're irrigating. Where's all the water coming from?"

Bastards. They couldn't get away with this. It was selfish

DOWN THE RABBIT HOLE

and destructive to the environment and other farmers. Funding was provided by the government to help farmers build dams with the intention that farmers would modernise their farming systems. Water entitlements could then be returned. Returning water entitlements would mean healthier river systems. Instead, these people were water pirates, pillaging the system.

"I reported it, but nothing came of it."

My eyes widened. He reported them? Farmers never reported one another, even anonymously. It was some sort of boy's club where they all stuck together, or turned a blind eye, no matter what the wrongdoing.

Before I could ask, he interrupted my thoughts with a curt "Best you get your bags out of the kitchen. You know where your room is."

Then he stood and walked to the railing effectively dismissing me. I sighed. I needed to be grateful that we'd had a conversation, not think about how abruptly it finished.

This was exactly what it was like growing up. I was always dismissed. After dinner I'd spent hours in my room alone. There was no family discussion, no watching TV together...no *anything* together. The only time we really talked was when Luke was with us. That was the only time I didn't feel lonely. I walked to my room, fighting off those memories, ignoring the lost feeling trying to invade my heart.

EARLY MORNINGS WERE the way of life on a farm, and I still stuck with them.

My room hadn't changed. Brown carpet stretched to the

window on the opposite side of the room. My mum had joked when I was young and continually traipsed mud through the house, that she'd chosen the right colour. I sat at my small desk. The cream wall above it, once plastered in nature posters, was empty. It left me feeling the same.

There were a few emails I could reply to straight away. Others required a more in-depth response. Before I closed the lid to my laptop, I messaged my brothers and sister to update them. Maybe they'd surprise me and actually respond, or even better, call Dad.

Dad was still in bed when I was ready to go into town. I didn't want to disturb him, but I didn't want to leave without seeing him either. I walked to his room and paused outside the door. I curled and uncurled my fingers, not knowing if I had the strength to knock. This was ridiculous. He was my father. I raised my hand and knocked.

"Dad?" I called out softly as I opened the door.

No response. I stepped into the room. "Dad?"

He stirred under the covers, then opened his eyes and looked at me.

I stood there not wanting to go any further. He rolled onto his side and sat up, his legs hanging over the side. Did he need help getting up? Should I offer to help him? What if he shrugged me off like he did yesterday? I didn't have Luke here to help with the hurt. I stood, waiting, watching.

"I'm going into town now. Is there anything you'd like me to get for you?"

He rubbed his eyes. "Milo."

My chest squeezed. "You want Milo?"

"Isn't it your favourite drink?"

He remembered.

"Yes." My voice sounded funny to my ears.

"Well, I guess you'll be staying a while, so you should at least have your favourite drink."

Warmth radiated through my body. Milo was one of the few extras we were allowed as children, even though I was the only one who liked it.

"And Tim Tams. Multiple packets."

Milo and Tim Tams. Wow, we were going all out. I added them to the mental list I had of the ingredients for his favourite meals.

"Do you need any help before I go?"

"No, I should be right."

I guess I really had no choice but to trust him. He had no reason to lie.

"OK. I won't be long."

"It's OK. I can manage."

I nodded and walked out of the room.

"Don't you let them give you shit," he called after me.

LUKE and I grabbed our bags ready to head to the change room. Before we could say goodbye to our parents Bianca's voice drifted to us. "I can't believe they let her play. Football isn't a girl's game."

"She's such a drongo if she thinks she can keep up in a real game. She'll cop it out there," Corey said. "She'd never be allowed on our team."

"Show pony. Look she's even in boy's shorts."

"And compression shorts."

"Because her legs are so fat." Bianca giggled.

Idiots. They had nothing to do with my fat legs. Half the players wore them to stop chafing.

Luke and I rolled our eyes. Dad grabbed my wrist and pulled me towards him. "Don't let them give you shit."

I nodded and followed Luke.

Coach had warned me that I'd be a target. Corey made sure of it.

Within the first few minutes of the game Luke had the ball. We were on the fourth tackle and thirty metres out from our line. He looked around for someone to pass it to. I ran forward. Because I was one of the fastest players on the team I played on the wing. Luke spotted me coming up from behind and passed the ball. I caught it with steady hands in mid stride and picked up speed. Players thundered after me. Twenty-five metres. Twenty. Ten. I kept an eye on my teammates. I needed to know where they were in case I needed to pass.

Five metres.

Someone was close. When I heard the word 'bitch' I knew it was Corey.

One metre.

My head was wrenched back. He had hold of my ponytail. I was yanked off my feet and thrown to the ground, his momentum pushing us forward. I wasn't close enough to the line to get a try, so I held onto the ball for dear life, crashing into the ground with it safe in my hands. Corey came down on top of me. All seventy kilos of him. His elbow digging into my back. I swear it hit with such force my ribs bent around the ball I held close to my chest.

All that mattered was I still had the ball.

"Get off her, you fucking prick," Luke yelled.

Corey dug his elbow in and planted his other hand on my

cheek grinding my face into the ground. His weight was lifted off. I moved my head to the side to see what was happening. A couple of teammates were holding Luke back. His face reddening as he yelled and struggled to get free.

A whistle sounded. I turned my head to the referee and thought about getting up. My energy was sapped, and pain hit every time I moved. The referee pulled a red card from his pocket and pointed it at Corey. He just smirked.

"Totally worth it," he said as he walked off the field.

Luke stared after him, murder in his eyes.

"Can't believe you held onto the ball," our forward said to me.

I nodded and accepted his hand.

At half time I left the change room and went to Dad's car. He kept a pocketknife in the glove box. I wasn't going to be a target anymore. My hair was a weakness. I grabbed hold of my ponytail and hacked it off.

When Dad saw it later, he smiled, ruffled up my hair and said, "That's my girl."

MRS PHILLIPS and Corey watched me as I walked into the rural supplies. I checked out the pallets of seed on my way to the hardware section. They had enough for what I needed. I grabbed two padlocks and some chain and made my way to the counter. They eyed them as I placed the items down.

"Locking something up?" Corey asked.

More like out, but yeah, whatever.

"Just need to make some things secure."

Like our privacy and sanity.

"Right. Wouldn't think there'd be anything worth taking out there."

Arsehole. He was as bulky as he was when we were teens, but it had changed from muscle to fat. He was lucky that he was tall so it was well distributed. Mrs Phillips stood next to her son; her nose turned up.

"I'd like to grab twenty bags of French White Millet too, please."

"We don't have any."

"There are twenty on a pallet over there."

"They're for someone else."

I took a breath in. "Can you order some in for me please?"

"Nah. The supplier's run out." He stared at me.

"The supplier's run out?"

"Yeah."

I pushed the chain and padlocks towards them.

"I'll just take these thanks."

"No problem. Gotta keep your shit safe."

"I'm sure it will do its job keeping intruders out." I eyed Mrs Phillips making sure she knew I was speaking about her.

I ENTERED Brodsky's Rural in the next town over. I'd phoned them on my forty-minute drive to make sure they had stock. A short lady behind the counter smiled as I approached. Relief flooded through me. Finally, someone nice.

"Hi, I'm Emily Watson. I called about the millet seed."

"Emily Watson? *The* Emily Watson?"

I cocked my head. What did she mean by that? I rested my hands against my thighs.

"I'm not sure if I'm *the* Emily Watson."

"Sure you are. I recognise you. You're the girl from Alma who's given new life to sustainable farming, who knows what it's like to be a farmer and gives sensible, practical advice. That Emily Watson." All the words tumbled out at a hundred miles an hour.

I laughed. What on Earth? "Yes, I'm that Emily Watson."

"I'm honoured to meet you. My husband and I have been following you forever." She looked over towards a man in the loading dock. "Bruce, Bruce, come here. You'll never believe who this is."

Bruce ambled over, his brown eyes peering at me.

"It's Emily Watson," his wife said, bouncing from foot to foot and nodding at me. The couple were my father's age. I shook my head, a bemused smile on my face.

Bruce stuck out his hand. "It's a pleasure to meet you, Miss Watson."

I shook it. "How do you know who I am?"

"Eleven years ago, a sales rep came in here after a meeting at the Alma District Farmers Co-op. He raved about a young girl named Emily Watson. He said that one day you'd change the world of farming and would put him out of a job," Bruce said.

That fateful meeting had set my course for the future and hammered a nail in the 'Hate Emily' coffin. The farmers thought I was trying to show them up, that I thought they were stupid, that I was better than them. All I wanted was for them to listen.

"We watched out for you after that," his wife said. "Our twins went to high school with you."

Twins? "Oh, you're Callum and Dustin's parents."

She nodded. "They competed against you in the Rural Schools Agricultural Competition. Your entry was about cover crops. It was so well thought out and we were impressed when you got advice from the university about how to set up the experiment."

"Our boys were spewing, weren't they, Susie? They thought there was no way their entry on pest management solutions would lose." Bruce laughed. "Until you came along."

That entry was another nail in the 'Hate Emily' coffin.

"We loved listening to you talk at the district show. Your enthusiasm really hit a note with us," Susie said.

And another nail.

"It was no surprise to us when you were offered that scholarship." She looked at her husband who nodded.

The final nail.

"Let's just say we've been watching, listening and learning from you for a very long time," Bruce said. He laughed, a deep belly laugh. "Now it sounds like we're stalking you."

"We're pleased your business is such a success and you've been able to help so many farmers."

I blushed. "Thank you. It helps when you have a team with the same vision."

Susie indicated to a pallet of seed. "Emily is here to buy some French Millet seed."

"Didn't they have any stock in Alma?"

"They had stock but wouldn't sell it to me."

Bruce shook his head. "I'm not surprised. They're still as

resistant to change as they've always been. We welcome your business anytime."

I smiled at him. The tightness which had been in my shoulders in Alma was gone.

"Are you staying long? Maybe you could give a talk at our farming co-op meeting?" Bruce asked.

"Would you? It would be the highlight of the year," Susie said.

Give a talk? Here? I bit my lip. I suppose it wouldn't be like giving a talk in Alma. Bruce and Susie had made me feel welcome the moment I'd come into the store, but it didn't mean everyone would. Not only that, I was here to look after my father, anything else would have to come second.

"I'll see what I can do." I pulled a business card out of my purse. "Email me the dates and let me know what you'd like me to talk about."

Susie smiled as big as a kid who'd found out the school bus had broken down.

CHAPTER EIGHT

Luke

Everyone turned to watch as Mum and I entered the meeting hall, with furtive glances to Mrs Phillips and then back to us. Their hushed talk filled the room. I moved toward the back, where we usually sat. The hall was stuffy, filled with more bodies than had been present at previous meetings. Mrs Phillips smiled and swept her way across the room to us, as if she were gliding across a dance floor. I was taken aback when she blocked our path.

"Luke, Bernie, how nice to see you here." She took hold of my arm and held it like we were the closest of friends.

It wasn't a surprise that we were here. We attended most meetings, not that we enjoyed them much. The other farmers mostly complained about how hard done by they were, but we did get some important information like expected rainfall, product information and market conditions. And it was important to maintain a connection to the community.

"Thanks," I said, glancing at Mum. I don't know what

reaction I was expecting from her, but the amusement in brown her eyes wasn't it.

"Thanks for your gracious welcome, Eleanor."

Eleanor considered Mum, the tiniest crease forming between her eyebrows.

Mum's gaze didn't falter. "Best we take our seats now."

I studied Mum closely. She wasn't usually so formal. She didn't wait for Mrs Phillips to answer but took my arm from her and moved into her seat, pulling me behind her. Mrs Phillips watched as we left her. She watched until we sat. Then she turned on her heel and made her way to the front of the room.

"You're not usually so slow on the uptake," Mum said loud enough for only me to hear.

"What?"

"Emily. This is all because of Emily."

"They can't be serious. She's here to look after Jim."

I glanced around the room. More than once I found people watching us. I shifted in my seat, heat rushing through my body, my face warming. These people were the reason she'd left in the first place. The reason I'd never had a chance with her. I still didn't have one, but there was no way I was going to let them ruin her time with Jim.

"You know what they're like," Mum said.

"Stupid, is what they're like."

"Luke don't let your anger win. We need to figure out what they're up to, not block them out."

I took a deep breath. And another. The oxygen lightened my limbs and cleared my head. I nodded to Mum. She was right.

Mum gave me a nudge and a sideways smile. "You make

me laugh. Emily is the only person who can get this reaction from you."

I shrugged. Emily caused lots of reactions from me. Most of which I couldn't act on. She had her life, I had mine. The most I could hope for was our continuing friendship. What I could *dream* about was a lot more than friendship and involved a whole load of nakedness. And touching. And sex. And—I really should not be thinking about these things around my mum.

Mum turned to me. "I don't know why—"

"Welcome to this month's meeting," Mrs Phillips started. "We've got some important things to discuss."

Murmurs erupted around the room. My stomach churned.

"Let's start with the elephant in the room, Emily Watson."

No fucking around for these people. Mum patted my leg. People started talking all at once. I tried to decipher their words but only caught them here or there. Back. Change. Crazy. Get rid of her. I clenched my teeth. They knew why she was here, but their backward arsed closed minds wouldn't let them see past their prejudice.

"OK. OK. Let's all calm down. Why don't we ask those closest to her what we need to know? Luke, Bernie, what is Emily doing here?"

Mum sat up straight. She ignored all the faces looking at her and addressed Mrs Phillips directly. "Jim is dying. Emily is here to look after him." Mum's voice had a distinct edge of sarcasm. I chewed the inside of my cheek to stop my smile. So much for not letting anger win.

"If she's here looking after Jim, why is she buying seed?"

"To combat the weeds on the farm." Mum's derisive tone was clear, as if she was speaking to the most ignorant people on Earth. This wasn't going to help. I tapped her foot with mine. It was enough for her to come back to herself.

Before Mum spoke again, I shifted in my chair and gazed around the room, making eye contact with the farmers. Mum did the same. "Jim didn't plant a crop this year. He was too sick. Weeds have started to grow in the fields. Emily is buying seed to plant a cover crop."

The returning voices were clearer now. They each took their turn.

"She could just spray."

"That's what we'd do."

I shook my head. She was nothing like these people. She never would be.

"I don't know why she's even bothering."

"Unless she's planning to stay."

Here? With you lot? Never. I ground my teeth. This, them, their attitude, had put a stop to our future together before it even started.

"We don't want her type here."

"No tree huggers."

"They'll rip our water allocations away."

"Yeah, she'll be in the government's ear saying they let us have too much water."

I took a deep breath. Idiots. "Emily is not going to stay. She has a business to return to."

"We know what her business does. We don't need that shit here."

"She'll try to change us. For her business."

As if she would waste her time on these people. In some

areas around Australia over ninety percent of the farmers used no till farming, but farmers here in Alma wouldn't even consider it. Same with cover crops. The reason? Ignorance. Not that they had a reason to be ignorant, they'd had Emily here for years.

"Emily is here to look after her father. That's all. She will be too busy with that and their farm to worry about you," I said. Why couldn't they just leave her alone and let her spend time with Jim in peace? That's all she wanted to do.

"She tried to change us eleven years ago."

"She'll try again. We don't need her greenie rubbish."

These people were ridiculous. They had their heads so far up their arses they couldn't even hear what I was saying. I wanted to smash their heads together. Instead, I repeated myself, "Emily is not interested in changing you."

"Bullshit."

Mrs Phillips voice sounded over the crowd. She smiled. She'd got the reaction she'd wanted. "Luke, I think we need someone to keep a close eye on her."

The energy changed in the room as people shifted in their seats, nodding in agreement.

"Luke, we need you to watch her, learn what she is doing and report back."

Cold spread though me. They couldn't be serious. "You want me to spy on her?"

Mum moved beside me. Her face was set in a hardened stare. It wouldn't be hard to see what Emily was up to, I'd be with her as much as I could. Report it back to them? Not unless I told her first. I would never lie to Emily.

"Yes, that's exactly what we want. Thanks, Luke. We knew we could count on you."

I hadn't even agreed. This was ridiculous. How could a whole community be suspicious of one young woman? And now they were just going to start the same bullshit all over again?

I wouldn't be a part of it...but...maybe if they think I'll do it, they'll leave Emily alone.

CHAPTER NINE

Emily

"Are you sure you know how to do this?" Luke asked.

I was about to climb up into the tractor that the single disc seeder was hooked up to. I gave him a sideways glance and then waved my hand in front of my face and fluttered my lids. "Oh Luke, I don't think I can. This machine is just too big for me to handle. Would you save me?"

He rolled his eyes.

"Oh, but Luke. You are such a big strong man and I'm so small and well, such a girl, I can't possibly do this without you. I need your manliness." I gave my best ditzy female performance as I looked him up and down. "All of your manliness."

"You're an idiot." He chuckled.

I had to avert my eyes when I thought of his manliness. There was no way I was looking *there*. I took a breath and turned on him, hands on my hips. "I'm hands-on in my business. I've driven machinery since I left the farm."

"Yeah, but cars don't count." He smirked at me. Smart

arse was reeling me in. That smile could reel in more than just my reaction. It pulled on my heart as well.

He looked at me, seriousness written on his face. "You know we've started CTF, so you'll need to keep the wheels on the wheel tracks."

"I'm sure I can manage." I wasn't rising to his teasing again. I didn't know Dad had started with any of these techniques. The controlled traffic farming meant the vehicles travelled on permanent wheel tracks separated from the crop growing areas. It could reduce wheel traffic by over fifty percent. The soil where the crops grew wasn't compacted by the wheels, allowing the plants better access to water. By not tilling the soil and using controlled traffic farming, farmers could gain 75mm more soil moisture.

"If you say so," he said.

I looked up at the cab. "Do you want to come up with me?"

He grinned, his eyes lighting up and made his way to the steps. "I thought you'd never ask."

I shook my head at him. He just couldn't help himself.

We followed track after track as the seed was planted. Luke told me how the two farms shared machinery and how they'd worked together to calculate the measurements for the tracks. His voice was full of excitement as he spoke about wheels and machinery widths being aligned.

Not being built for two, the cab was a bit squishy. I was aware of how close Luke was as his thigh pressed against mine and his heat seeped into me. His earthiness filled the cabin. Breathing it in made my whole body aware of him. The energy was like when you turned on a string of Christmas lights and the globes lit up one after another. When we turned at the end of the row, he rested his hand on my shoulder for balance. His hand was warm, strong, and oh so close to my breast. My stupid nipples hardened in response. It would be easier if I sat on his knee but just the thought of being that much closer to him made my insides tremble. Not going to happen.

Instead of thinking about how close Luke was and how absurd my thoughts were, I concentrated on what he was saying about his work at the wildlife refuge. He'd volunteered there since we were young teens.

The tractor had electronic guidance, so it didn't require much concentration on my part. I only needed to keep the correct speed, turn at the end of the rows, and make sure I followed the guidance system, which was more like lane departure systems in cars than automatic steering.

When we were finished, we headed back to the machinery shed.

"Do you want me to back the seeder in?" Luke asked.

"Are you saying I can't do it?" I knew that wasn't what he was saying. He was a hands-on man, and he was itching to do something. I waited for his answer.

"That's not what I meant. You're fully capable."

"Just making sure." I smiled up at him. "OK. Let's swap spots."

I stood up to move around him. Luke moved closer. He held onto my hips as he manoeuvred himself onto the seat. Even after he was seated, he held on. Heat spread from his hands to my stomach. I imagined him pulling me down and kissing me like I'd never been kissed before. I moved away, breaking the contact. I didn't know where to look.

"I'll get down and unhitch when you're done."

I scrambled down off the tractor. I was unprepared for these feelings I was having for Luke. Being near him had my body responding in ways it shouldn't. I'd squashed those feelings a long time ago. Luke wasn't interested in me in that way, and that was OK. We had our friendship and that's what counted.

I watched Luke back the seeder in. It was a tight squeeze, but he managed with ease. It was pure skill. I moved forward and unhitched the tractor. I waved up at Luke to let him know he was loose. The distance between us made me brave and I was able to look up at him and smile.

"How did I do?" he called down to me.

I shrugged. He knew he was good and didn't need me to tell him.

"Aw, come on. You gotta give me some credit."

"Fine. You did an amazing job."

"Is that all you've got for me?"

"Just go park the tractor. I'll go get lunch ready."

That man cracked me up. I wasn't about to shower him in compliments. I knew where that would lead. He would add it to his list of 'boyfriend material' qualities. Joking, of course. I didn't need reminding about how perfect he was. I knew that list by heart. There was one failure—he couldn't be my boyfriend.

But I didn't want him to be anyone else's either.

And with that boyfriend perfection list, I was surprised he hadn't been snapped up already. I shook my head, dreading the thought, and walked to the house.

"All done?" Dad asked from the verandah as I walked up the stairs.

"Yes."

"Good job."

Happiness spread through my chest. "Thanks. The guidance system works well."

I leant against the door not wanting the conversation to end. If I didn't move, maybe he'd continue to talk like he had the other day. I was eager to listen to anything he had to say.

"Luke did most of the work setting up the wheel tracks. He changed out the axles on the harvester to get the wheels in the right position."

"Better than buying a new one."

"Yeah. We needed to invest in the disc seeder so that was enough to outlay."

Luke approached. Tall, tanned, with an easy gait. I tried to keep my eyes off him, but it was hard. His blond hair and warm brown eyes always drew me in. What was wrong with me? I turned my attention back to Dad.

"What else did you do to get it all set up?"

"Extended the arms on some of the machinery. It resulted in having to do less runs which meant fewer wheel tracks and more land for harvesting."

I'd implemented similar systems on other farms. All the mathematical equations gave the brain a good workout. I'm sure Luke would excel at it. He had one of those logical minds.

"I should get you on our team," I said to Luke as he walked up the stairs.

His eyebrows knitted together. "I am on your team."

My heart smiled.

"I meant the Land Reinvigorated team."

He cocked his head.

"Dad says you did all the set up here for the controlled traffic farming."

Luke blushed. "It wasn't just me. Our parents helped as well."

Dad interrupted. "Don't be modest. He worked on it at night and in the morning he'd show us the plans. Steve and I would think he was done but then he'd do more research and come up with a better plan."

"It was only looking at machinery and stuff. Not rocket science." Luke shifted from foot to foot and looked down at the weathered boards beneath them. I'd never seen him so self-conscious before.

Dad looked pointedly at me. I was so onboard with this idea that if I was a stowaway, even the captain wouldn't be able to throw me off the ship. I imagined being able to spend time with him in person after I left. Working beside him, being close to him, feeling his warmth...For goodness' sake, I needed to stop this way of thinking.

"No rocket scientists on my team. We need people with their feet planted firmly on the ground."

Luke's eyes met mine. I held my breath. I wanted this more than anything I'd wanted in a long time. I hoped he wouldn't discount my idea. His pause made me realise that he wouldn't want to leave the farm.

"You could be a consultant. That way you could work on the farm and be a part of my team."

A part of me knew I was being selfish, wanting to use his skills so I could spend time with him. But it wasn't just about me. This would show Luke how important he was. He always thought there was nothing for him but the farm. That's where his contribution started and finished. There was nothing wrong with that; farming was a noble profession. Without farmers, we would die. I knew a part of him wanted more. Not a whole new life more, but something a little extra. Maybe I could give it to him.

Luke nodded. "That might work."

CHAPTER TEN

Luke

I THOUGHT about Emily's offer on my way home. Her business made an important contribution to society. I'd always wanted to be a part of that. I'd often thought about expanding on it, concentrating on building wildlife corridors and reintroducing native wildlife into those areas. That would be my ideal, my way of making an important contribution to the world. I couldn't though. Not when I was destined to take over the farm.

And I couldn't walk away from it. My parents worked hard to make the farm a success, always with the intent of passing it onto me. I loved the farm as much as I loved them. Maybe we were so close because I was an only child. Maybe it was because I knew how much heartbreak they went through trying to have a child for over fifteen years. Whatever it was, I never wanted to disappoint them and leaving the farm was sure to be a disappointment.

Her offer was hard to knock back. She believed in me as much today as she had when we were younger.

"*I'M TOO STUPID,*" I said, throwing the pencil down.

Emily moved it back onto the problem sheet, then took my hand.

"Luke." She didn't continue talking until I looked at her. My face was hot. "You are not stupid. You are one of the smartest people I know."

"If I'm so smart, why did Miss Srang, drop me back two classes in maths?"

"Sometimes you need to go backwards to move forwards. I do it all the time."

That was a load of crap. Emily never went backwards. She nodded at me.

"When I read some articles, they talk about things I've never heard of. I need to go back to basics and work my way forward. Every time I go back to basics, I learn more, I remember more."

I looked down at the page, at the equations that may as well have been written in another language.

"We will go backwards as far as we need to. Something will click, Luke."

We worked together day after day. Every day she told me I could do it, that I could achieve anything. She worked with me, helped me through, and when I came out the other side, I was one of the best maths students in class.

She never made me feel any less than her. If it wasn't for her, I would have been a ball of frustration. I would have given up. It was her belief in me that kept me going.

. . .

"YOU'RE HOME EARLY," Dad said as I walked into the shed. He was measuring up some stair treads on the saw bench.

"Emily had work to do on a couple of proposals."

"She's a busy girl—working on the farm, looking after Jim, getting the house in order and working in her business."

This would be a good time to talk to him about Emily's proposal. I was excited about the prospect.

He glanced at me before marking out a cut line. "I guess you'll be over there a lot."

"Yeah." There was no way I was missing out on spending time with Emily. She would never come back after Jim died. Anyone would have thought it would be strange spending time with each other every day after being separated for all these years. It was just like it had been before she'd left—easy, normal, fun.

"Nothing's changed." He smiled at me. Before I could respond, he slid his safety glasses down over his twinkling blue eyes and dropped the saw onto the wood.

The shrillness of the saw only lasted a moment. I grabbed the length he'd cut, and he moved the remainder of the plank in line to cut. I'd have to get measurements for Jim's stairs so we could at least repair that bottom step. We should get a ramp ready, too. He would need it when he started using the wheelchair full time.

"Spending all that time there will help you with your spy duties."

Mum had told him.

"Ha ha. Funny."

65

"I'm not the one who agreed to it."

"I didn't agree either."

"Not declining their offer is *agreeing* to it, you know?"

I shook my head. The whole thing was stupid. As if I'd tell them anything about Emily.

"Have you told Emily?"

"Not yet. She hates this place as it is, and I don't want her to feel worse."

I couldn't make eye contact with Dad. Instead, I stared down at the wood.

"Is that the only reason?"

"I guess not. I don't want her to be angry with me either."

"The longer you leave it the more risk of that happening."

"I know, but it's not like I'm actually going to spy."

"Luke—"

"Just cut the wood already."

He was right. I did need to tell her. She deserved to know. Not just about the spying but also about how everyone had acted at the meeting. I just needed the right moment; when I wasn't confused about my feelings. It was a lame excuse, and I knew it. We'd had such a good morning working together, talking and joking. It was weird. I'd lived without her by my side for so many years, hardly seeing her in person, but now she was back, touching her was like a drug. The hug, her nudges, that moment in the tractor. Holy hell, if she hadn't moved, I would have pulled her into my lap and kissed her. I imagined her straddling me, her chest pushed against mine while we kissed. My dick going hard beneath her. Even now...

"Luke."

Shit, I was on my way to a full-blown fantasy in front of my dad. With my face burning hot, I glanced at him.

"Can you take the wood?"

"Oh yeah, sorry."

I tried not to laugh at the mention of wood or the prospect of taking it. I took a deep breath and made sure I was no longer in fantasy land.

"Emily made me an offer earlier."

Dad headed to another plank and I helped him lift it onto the bench. I should have been here to help him lift the last one.

"Oh yeah, what sort of offer?" He gave me a sideways smile. I was surprised he didn't nudge me and give me a wink. I rolled my eyes at him.

"Jim was telling her about my work on getting the new traffic system in place. She asked if I'd like to work for her business. As a consultant."

Dad was quiet as he measured up the wood. I ran my hand through the blond hair I'd inherited from him and waited for him to say something.

"So, she's planning to steal my best worker?" He didn't look at me as he marked the next cut line.

"It won't be full time. As a consultant I can choose when I work."

Had I made a mistake telling him before I'd decided? Would he try to talk me out of it?

"So, in the off season or when we have down time?"

"Yeah, exactly."

He nodded before moving the wood into position and cutting it.

This was totally doable...I think.

CHAPTER ELEVEN

Emily

Dᴀᴅ and I walked into the specialist department at the hospital. Luckily, we could park in the disabled spot and the doors were close. Dad declined his wheelchair every day saying he would keep walking while he could. The department was painted a pale blue-green, bringing serenity to the space. The furniture was all light and gave off the same vibe.

I'd avoided hospitals as much as I could since the accident. It was an isolating place for me. One which only brought back bad memories. My physical state when I'd left was good. I'd been a normal kid with a few scars and an injured brain which had recovered. On the inside, I was different. The loss I felt, I attributed to that place.

I stood off to the side as Dad approached the counter.

"Good morning, Jim," the nurse said full of cheer and sunshine. The man was dying, and she radiated happiness. Weird.

"Hi, Delores."

"Take a seat. Dr Hans will be with you shortly."

The nurse glanced at me. Her eyes widened. She smiled. Not just a hello kind of smile but a holy moly, this is amazing kind of smile. I took a small step back. She came around the counter, her energy hardly contained in her round body.

"This must be Emily. She looks so much like you Jim," she gushed. I stood, transfixed, as she took my hands. "I've heard so much about you. Your dad didn't talk much when he first came in." Her eyes flitted to Dad and then straight back to me. "You know, the silent, brooding type. It must have been the second or third treatment. Was it the third, Jim?"

Dad nodded. The rambling woman was crazy. He didn't seem to notice. They let nurses like this near patients? Dying patients?

"Yes, the third. That's when I tried to break down those walls. I asked about his children. I don't know if it was the drugs or if I hit some magic button, but he wouldn't shut up about you."

OK. This was weird. I wanted to step away, but I couldn't. She still had hold of my hands. I glanced at Dad who stood dead still beside me.

"Every fortnight we heard a different story. Luke or Bernie would sit by and laugh with us as he spoke of your antics. How you chopped off your hair at the football. How you climbed a tree and slept up there so your dad wouldn't cut it down, until he convinced you it was sick and had to go. Even then, you would only come down when he agreed to plant seven in its place. One for each of your family, and one for Luke."

OK. This woman was certifiable. Breathing seemed to be an option for her. I turned to Dad for help. He shrugged. He wouldn't make eye contact and he was blushing. This was all too weird.

"It was always Luke. He was always there with you. Oh, he is such a nice young man. Kind. Warm. If I was twenty years younger, you'd have to watch out for me."

I narrowed my eyes at the folly of her words. "What?"

"I would fight you for him."

Fight me for Luke? Luke wasn't mine.

"OK, Delores. I think you're scaring her." Dad's tone was amused but held enough seriousness for Delores to stop talking. She looked down at our entwined hands. Her hands withdrew so quickly mine almost followed in their powerful wake.

"Oh. Yes. Right." She straightened her clothing and smoothed it down. Serious now, she considered me. "I'm sorry, Emily. You must think I'm crazy."

I shook my head. I doubt I was convincing.

"I feel like I've known you forever. Your dad's stories were just mesmerising."

"Thank you." It wasn't even an appropriate response, but I couldn't think of anything else to say.

Dad tugged on my arm and I followed him to the seating area.

"I have to get weighed and get some blood taken by the nurse. I'll be back soon."

I sat and watched as a new patient approached the desk. Delores was much more subdued with this one. Maybe I'd judged her too quickly. Maybe she wasn't crazy after all. She caught me watching and gave me a small smile. My face reddened. She had a different demeanour with each person. Amazing that she chose exuberant with my dad. My dad who'd spoken about me fortnight after fortnight.

Spoke about *me*.

Dad sat down beside me. "Delores isn't crazy. She just knows her patients. She's not happy that I'm dying, just happy that I'm still here."

Tears sprung into my eyes. She was happy Dad was here. So was I. Time, as limited as it was, was all we had left. Time to heal. These things he spoke about with her were not things we reminisced about at home as if they were fond memories or something to be proud of. Once they were done, they were not spoken about again. So why was he talking to Delores about them like they were something special?

I smiled then shook my head. How could I be special enough to talk about when all he wanted me to do was leave? It didn't make sense.

"Jim Watson," a male voice called out.

Dad stood and I followed him into a consultation room. It was plainly furnished with a bed, desk and two chairs. The doctor shook Dad's hand and gave him a larrikin smile. Then he clasped mine in both of his. Seriously, again?

"You must be Emily. It's a pleasure to meet you."

I squinted at him. "I'm not Emily."

He dropped my hands as quick as a city person would drop manure.

"I'm sorry. I just thought..."

Dad burst out laughing. The doctor looked between us.

"She's joking, Hans."

"Like father, like daughter," he said, joining his laughter. "Your dad is full of jokes just like this."

I smiled. "Sorry, I couldn't help myself."

The doctor, Hans, pointed us to our seats. "How have you been feeling, Jim?"

"For someone who's dying, I'm doing OK."

Seriously?

"Well, that's positive. How's the pain level?"

"So far, so good."

Enough already.

"Dad," I said, my voice stern. How could he be so complacent about it all? I watched out all the time for changes. Even the smallest, insignificant ones had me panicking. I didn't want to think about what each change meant or start counting down the months or weeks, but I found I was anyway.

"Fine. I've started to feel some discomfort. I'm taking half a tablet to help with it."

"Do you take half every four hours?"

"No, just when I feel I need it."

"Good. Good."

I sighed. Something positive from the doctor.

"Appetite?"

"Not bad. Emily's a good cook so that helps."

This was surreal. Dad talking about me to others. Dad complimenting me. Dad having a sense of humour. I'd missed that about him. When I was little, he laughed and joked a lot, and teasing us kids had been a favourite pastime of his.

"Lethargy?"

"Not bad."

I wanted to give the doctor some context, hoping for another positive comment. "He's awake most of the morning."

"Got to keep an eye on you and Luke," Dad said.

What on Earth was he talking about? "I'm pretty sure you can trust us."

"With the farm work maybe." What was that in his voice? Sly humour?

Hans chuckled. I'm surprised they didn't high five each other.

On our way out I made sure I stopped at the nurse's desk. I wanted to reassure Delores that she hadn't tormented me. She turned to me and smiled. Not her the-sky-is-blue-and-the-sun-is-shining smile, a small hesitant smile.

Giving her a smile of my own, I said, "It was nice to meet you, Delores. We'll see you in a few weeks."

Bam. The smile beamed.

"You too, Emily. You keep hold of that man now. Good ones are hard to find."

CHAPTER TWELVE

Luke

"Do you need anything from town? The parts for the tractor have come in," I said to Mum.

"Yes, please. I'll write a list. I'd like to make a casserole for Emily. She works so hard."

"That's nice of you, Mum."

"Well, she's not used to cooking for three. I guess with the amount Jim eats he doesn't count as a whole person. Though you probably make up for that."

I hadn't thought of that. So much had changed for Emily in such a short time. She usually lived alone, meaning she had her own space and didn't need to share. She worked in an office instead of at her desk in her old room. When she cooked it was only her she had to worry about. Since being back she split her time between the farm, Jim, and work. So many changes, so much sacrifice and not once had I heard her complain.

"Here you go." Mum handed me the list.

I gave it a once over. I was a one stop shopper, so I was relieved to see that it could all be bought at the supermarket. "Do you need them in a hurry? I'm going into the refuge first to do a couple of hours there."

"No, you take your time. I'll have plenty of time to cook when you get home."

The wildlife refuge was my special place. It was where what I did benefited more than just me and the farm. It's where I did something I felt was worthwhile. I had Emily to thank for introducing me to it.

I HAD Emily by the hand and was running to the river. Emily was not a slow runner but at that moment in time I would have thought that Usain Bolt wasn't fast enough. As we got close to the spot I slowed down. Emily had no idea what I wanted to show her, but she didn't question me when I put my finger to my lips.

I pointed to the base of one of the trees. There was an injured possum staring at us, its leg and body cut. It stared at us with eyes so wide I thought they might pop out. I was sure it was young because it didn't seem to have grown into its ears yet.

Emily made her way toward it. I held her back.

"No, stop. It will be scared and might scratch you."

I should have asked her to bring a towel but hadn't thought of it. I took my t-shirt off and approached it slowly. The poor baby was so frightened it didn't move.

"It's OK baby. We're here to help you." My voice was low and soft. Even when I was centimetres from it, talking quietly, it didn't try to run. I placed my t-shirt over it and wrapped it as

carefully as I could. The poor baby was shaking, and I didn't know if it was fear or from being cold, so I did the only thing I could and held it to my chest. It didn't squirm or try to get away.

I walked home, cradling it, while Emily ran ahead to call the wildlife rescue. She ran back and told me their instruction was to take the baby to the vet. When I walked into the kitchen Mum went to take the baby from me. "The rescue said I should put it in a box so it's safe and secure."

As soon as I held it out to her the baby started shaking. I pulled it straight back to my chest where it settled.

Emily stepped forward. "The baby wants Luke."

"I need to take it to the vet," Mum said.

"Luke would like to go with you."

How did she know that?

"It's OK." Mum was using her soothing voice, for the baby possum or Emily I will never know. Probably both. "The baby will be safe with me."

"Luke is going with you," Emily said again, insistent. Before Mum had a chance to say otherwise Emily stalked off and returned with a new t-shirt for me. She took the baby from me so I could get dressed and then handed it back. Not once did she pay any attention to my mum.

When Mum and I got in the car, Mum said to me, "It's lucky I like that girl. Her bossiness is going to get her in trouble one day."

She liked Emily so much, in fact, that when Emily insisted I help with the possum's rehabilitation at the wildlife carer's, Mum agreed and took me twice a week. After the possum's release, she then asked Mum to drive me to the refuge once a week so I could volunteer. Mum agreed to that, too.

It was Emily's actions that made me realise how much I wanted to be involved in caring for wildlife. I was always drawn to it. We would stop by the trees on the way to the river so I could watch the possums and other animals. Emily was always patient as I studied the area. It was like she knew how important it was to me before I did.

I WALKED into the wildlife refuge and made my way to the outdoor enclosures. Robbie, the caretaker, was out there changing some branches over in the enclosures. I went over and picked up the discarded branches to take them to the waste pile.

Robbie turned to me and scratched his red beard. "Wasn't sure we'd see you much now that Emily is home."

"You can't get rid of me that easily." I hauled the branches away.

"How is she?" Robbie asked when I was back in earshot. He was in one of the macropod enclosures, the one for permanent residents. These animals couldn't be returned to the wild because of injuries. A blind kangaroo approached me and nudged my hand. I bent and stroked its neck; it's fur soft against my hardened farmers hands. Animals destined to return to the bush were not handled this way. We didn't want them to become too complacent around humans.

"Emily's good."

"I'm surprised she's not here with you. You two were inseparable."

"She had work to do. She has some research to do for a project she's working on."

He nodded and continued cleaning the water trough.

"She offered me a consultant position in her business."

Robbie's eyes lit up. "For wildlife?"

I shook my head.

"You haven't spoken to her about your ideas, have you?"

"No. Not really."

"At all?"

He and I had spoken about this many a time. Often, I let my dreams run away as I was caught up in his mutual excitement. It wasn't long before I remembered dreams and reality were two different things.

"She would support your idea. She has always supported you. She brought you here, didn't she?"

"I know she would. What's the point, though? I wouldn't be able to commit myself to it in the way I want to."

"Because of the farm."

"Because of the farm."

My strokes turned to scratches and the kangaroo leaned into me. Robbie finished off the trough and turned to me. "And we are back at the beginning."

"I know." I sighed. Nothing was going to change. "My parents built the farm up, working their hands to the bone so they could leave me something. I can't just tell them I don't want it."

Robbie was understanding as usual and didn't push me on it. It wasn't perfect but I tried to have both worlds by working on the farm and volunteering.

"At least I get to use your skills." He smiled. "Can you continue on building that new enclosure please?"

I nodded and made my way to the shed to grab the tools I needed.

I WALKED into the small supermarket and grabbed a basket. I didn't even make it to the fresh produce section before I was stopped by the owner. "Luke, how are you?"

"Good thanks."

I made to resume my shopping, but he kept talking. "What's been happening with Emily?"

I stiffened and turned to the middle-aged, overweight man. He wasn't even a farmer. What did it matter to him what Emily was doing? What did it matter to anyone? It was none of their business.

"Nothing much."

I grabbed the vegetables I needed and moved on. When I got to the register, I saw his wife was serving. Great. I emptied the basket without acknowledging her.

"Hi, Luke. How's your task for the co-op going?"

"Nothing to report."

I wished she'd scan the products faster. Nothing ever happened fast in Alma. Unless it was the Phillips pulling a swifty.

"I heard Emily was back to pressure the farmers into making changes. She wants to rip their water rights away."

Right now, I wanted to rip *them* all away.

"Emily is here to look after Jim. She's not concerned with the other farmers."

"Is that what she told you?"

"That's what I'm telling you."

"Don't trust her. She's conniving."

I took a deep breath. They had no idea what type of person Emily was. She was stubborn, a perfectionist and a control freak. She was also caring, considerate, and she always went out of her way to make me feel good about myself, like that crazy perfect boyfriend list she had going. If only she could see me as the perfect boyfriend. Conniving she was not. I paid, grabbed my shopping, and didn't look back

I pulled up in front of the rural supplies. I didn't want to go in. If the supermarket was bad, this would be horrendous. I wouldn't be lucky enough to get in and get out. I looked up at the heavens for strength. Maybe it wouldn't be as bad as I thought.

And then I heard Bianca's voice. "Luke."

She met me halfway to the counter. I turned my head to the side and breathed through my mouth. Her perfume was overwhelming. I much preferred Emily's simple coconut scent.

Bianca looped her arm around mine. "You made Mum really happy when you said you would spy on Lemony."

I tried to pull my arm away, but she held on tight. I picked up my pace instead. She kept up, her hips swinging, knocking against mine. Leach. When I stopped at the counter, I shrugged free. Mrs Phillips gave me that fake sweet smile she'd given to Emily the day she'd turned up at Jim's. This whole family made me cringe.

"Luke darling, so nice to see you."

I spoke as soon as she paused. "I'm here to pick up the parts I ordered for the tractor."

"They're right here."

She pulled her shoulders back and bent forward. I diverted my eyes. I was so over this family. She stood up and placed the parts on the counter. I wished she would just bring up the bill.

"How's Emily?"

"She's fine."

"What has she been up to?"

"Nothing much."

"Has she been asking about us?"

"Not at all."

I stood up straight and placed my hands on the edge of the counter.

"Has she talked about our farms?"

"No."

"Why is she here then?"

I gripped the counter with my fingertips. I didn't want her to see my full-blown frustration. "I've already told you. She is here to look after Jim. There's no point spying because she's not up to anything."

"We'll see about that."

Enough. I grabbed my wallet out of my pocket. "How much do I owe you for the parts?"

Mrs Phillips mouth was a thin line. Bianca's hand took hold of my upper arm and my skin crawled. Why couldn't she just leave me alone? I forced myself not to pull away.

"$145."

I pulled my card out and looked at the machine. Mrs Philips keyed something into the computer and the amount owing came up on the screen. I keyed my details in and counted the seconds. Too many seconds.

As soon as the receipt was printed, I grabbed the parts. The leach was still attached. I managed to get my arm free.

"We'll see you at the next meeting," Mrs Phillips said as I walked away. "You can report back then."

This was getting out of hand. These people were relentless.

What was I even doing? I couldn't do this to Emily. I needed to tell her. I don't even know why I hadn't told her yet, and the longer I let it go the more I risked.

CHAPTER THIRTEEN

Emily

Dad was sitting on the porch watching Luke and me work in the house yard. I'd put a blanket on a chair beside him in case he felt cold. Satisfied he was OK I turned to the job at hand.

Luke and I had planted the millet weeks ago and were now concentrating on getting the house yard in order. The lawn was out of control, spreading into the garden beds with the weeds, and shrubs were overgrown. I was pruning Mum's beloved rose bushes. Lucky it was winter, and it was the right time to prune. They would be flowering again in a few months. I remembered them in full bloom, the colour, the scent. Would I still be here then? I hoped so.

Luke was mowing. I enjoyed the rhythmic noise of the mower as it approached and then moved on. Loud, quiet, loud, quiet. Like my thoughts. My thoughts about Dad and my thoughts about Luke. I'd missed them both. I loved them both. Both were always unattainable.

Dad hadn't welcomed me with open arms, but he hadn't pushed me away either. I was surprised he had spoken about me so openly to others. And the impression I got was that he'd done it in a loving way. Otherwise, why had they been so happy to see me? I couldn't understand why he was so open with them but withdrawn from me all that time.

We'd found a workable routine. When Luke and I were outside he would sit on the porch watching us. When he napped, usually in the afternoon, I made phone calls, had meetings, and did computer work. Luke would go home then to work on his farm or to volunteer at the refuge but would be back in time for dinner.

Silence brought me out of my thoughts. I turned to see Luke getting off the mower.

"Shit," he said as he crouched down to look at something.

I walked over to him. "What happened? Has something broken?"

I caught movement from the verandah; Dad stood up and moved to the banister. Luke turned to me, holding something in his hands. A baby rabbit with brown flecked fur so tiny it could fit in the palm of his hand. Its ear was bleeding. On closer inspection, part of its ear was missing.

"I didn't see it," Luke said, his voice soft, his brown eyes wide. "I only noticed it after another one ran off."

"We should try to find its family."

"I doubt we'll find them now. They'll be long gone."

"If you put it down maybe it will run off to be with them."

Luke put the baby on the ground. It didn't move, not even its head or its ears.

"Bring it here," Dad said.

My heart thumped. My first thought was that he'd kill it,

farmers had a legal obligation to control rabbits. They were bad for both the environment and farms. The last I heard they cost agriculture nearly one billion dollars a year through crop destruction, soil erosion and control costs. But if he wanted it dead, he would have told us to do it. Luke took the precious parcel over to Dad, who sat back down in his chair. They stretched their hands out to each other and Dad clasped the baby in his shaking hands. Was that a side effect of the cancer or his developing weakness? He'd once had the steadiest hands I'd ever seen. I walked over.

"See how the bleeding is slowing? The vessels in its ear are constricting to reduce blood flow."

Its ears were so thin the sunlight shone through them. The blood was drying up already just like he said.

"Will it be OK to go back to its family?" I asked.

"No. He's in shock." Dad cupped his hand around the baby and held it to his chest. "He's too young to be on his own. He won't be able to regulate his body temperature yet."

Dad popped the rabbit into his polo shirt pocket. "Go finish off what you're doing. I'll look after him."

"You can't keep him," Luke said. "It's illegal."

"What are they going to do? Fine a dying man?"

"Around here, probably."

Dad looked between us. "The baby is in shock. It may even have internal injuries. Let's see if we can nurse it back to health before we worry about the legality of keeping him."

"OK." I shrugged. What else could we do? Letting it go would mean certain death. My stomach dropped. This little baby represented life and hope. There was no hope for Dad. Not the sort of hope I wanted. Every day I tried not to dwell on the time he had left. It was like his fire was going out, glowing embers blackening one at a time, until all that would be left was soulless ash.

I walked down the stairs. Dad was peeking into his pocket, a wistful smile on his face, a totally different man than the one who'd denied me.

I RAN AS FAST as my eleven-year-old legs could carry me across the fields, recalling the little balls of fluff. I imagined having a kitten of my own. Something to love and keep me company. Something to sleep with me at night and to share my secrets with. A kitten to show me love. For me to love. A kitten to help me survive in my dreary home.

"Dad, Dad, the stray cat that moved into Luke's shed had kittens," I yelled as I ran into the house, the screen door slamming behind me. Dad turned from the stove. "There are five. They're so small. Bernie said I could have one if you said it was OK."

"No."

My heart dropped.

"But why? It will be my cat. I'll look after it."

"I don't need to feed a useless animal."

"I'll pay for the food with my pocket money. I'll pay for everything."

Surely, he couldn't say no to that. I was good at saving. I could afford it.

"We don't need a useless animal here."

"But—"

Dad slammed the lid down on the pot and threw the wooden spoon into the sink. "I bloody well said no."

Crying, I ran to my room. Later my sister said, "I don't know why you expected anything different."

I GUESS I shouldn't have been surprised by Dad's actions back then, but I sure was now. I didn't know anything about looking after rabbits or baby rabbits for that matter, but he seemed to know a lot.

As we sat down for dinner Dad gave the baby some water from an eye dropper. It drank eagerly.

"Shorty is going to need some special food."

"Shorty? You've named the rabbit?" Luke asked.

I glanced at Luke across the table. He shook his head. I loved having him over for dinner, as much as I had while we were growing up. Just like we were all one family.

"Sure. What was I going to do? Keep calling him baby rabbit?"

Luke shrugged a shoulder. "Why Shorty?"

"He has one short ear."

"And where do you propose we get this special food from?" I asked, twirling spaghetti and sauce onto my fork.

"Probably the vet."

"So, you want me to go to a vet and tell them I need feed for a rabbit, which I'm keeping illegally? You know we can get a sixty thousand dollar fine?"

Dad rolled his eyes at me. Lucky I was in the middle of chewing or I might have choked.

"Don't be daft. I want you to tell him you have a baby hare."

Well, I guess that was logical. Hares weren't illegal.

Perhaps this tiny baby animal would bring us closer together. We would have something to bond over that we'd never had before. Maybe Dad would learn to show me the love he so freely shared with others. Did he share that love with me, and I just hadn't recognised it? Thinking back, I wondered if I'd misread all of his actions. There were a lot of times he was there to support me. They always came to me clearly. But what about the times I'd felt unwanted? I could try to dismiss them, but the feelings were real, and they still felt real. I battled them every day. I battled the fear that he would turn me away.

I nodded. A baby hare it would be. It looked like I would be going on a road trip tomorrow. I hoped Luke would come along. Spending time with him made me realise how much I'd missed being with him. Before I'd left for uni, we'd spent almost every day together. As I'd laid in bed at night during those first weeks away, wishing my best friend was with me, I'd reminded myself that he didn't belong with me. The farm was his life and future. When I looked across at him, that same realisation hit me. I swallowed the lump in my throat. He was the only man I ever imagined marrying and having children with. It was as impossible today as it was back then. I may as well enjoy the time I would have with him. In a few months, seeing him every day would all be over.

CHAPTER FOURTEEN

Luke

EMILY LOOKED OVER AT ME, her feet up on the dashboard. How many times had we driven like this together? Countless. Her bare tanned legs were like a beacon to me.

"Check out your farmers tan," I said, pointing down to where her tan stopped at the height of where her boots usually were. I fingered the smooth skin where the tan finished. As I turned my attention back to the road my hand glided up her leg and over her knee. I wanted to go further, all the way to the hem of her shorts, to reach under the hem, touch her. Heat spread through me and landed between my legs. I yanked my hand away. This was crazy. Insane. These feelings needed to stay locked up. My hands needed to be locked up. My dick, that needed to be locked up, too.

"I think Brodsky's Rural will have what we need," she said. Her tone showed no sign that my touch had any effect on her. Good. She would just think it was like every other time we touched as teenagers. Nothing but a touch best friends shared. I wanted so much more but she never did.

I nodded. That would be ideal. There was no way I wanted to go into Alma. Every time I stepped foot in town someone would grill me about Emily. If they saw us together, there would be stares and murmurs. I didn't want to subject Emily to that. She had enough to worry about. I should have told her about the farmer's co-op, but she was in a place of contentment. She and Jim were getting along well, and she enjoyed working on the farm. Not only that but her brothers and sister had responded to her message and each had called their dad. It had given her relief that they took the time to reconnect, even in such a small way. I didn't want to dampen her spirits and I didn't want to risk the time we were spending together. Guilt hit me. Was I withholding the truth for her or for me?

Emily and I walked into the shed side by side. A short lady approached us, her smile wide. They sure were friendly here.

"Hi Emily. It's great to see you again."

"Hi, Susie. Luke and I are after some guinea pig or rabbit food please. Something suitable for a hare."

"Sure. Sure. Over this way."

She didn't question us or probe. This wouldn't have happened in Alma. They would have asked a stack of questions like everything was their business and they were entitled to know. Truth be told, you were expected to tell them everything they wanted to know before they even asked.

I followed Emily and Susie to some shelving units holding all types of food. Susie left us so we could browse together. After we gave the vet a description of Shorty and his condition, the vet had said that since Shorty's eyes were open, he must be at least ten days old and that meant we could start giving him hard feed as well as the special milk the vet gave us.

"This one?" Emily passed me a bag of food.

I shook my head. "Do they have anything else? These pellets might be too big for him."

She grabbed a different bag and we headed to the counter. The guy standing there had an identical smile to Susie's—wide and toothy with a small gap between his middle teeth. He looked familiar.

"Hi, Emily. Luke," he said, giving me a small nod. His attention went straight back to Emily.

"Hi, Callum," Emily said. I didn't need to look at her to see she had a smile on her face. Her voice said it all. I clenched my teeth. Callum. He and his brother had gone to high school with us. I recalled they'd entered a competition in their senior year with Emily. They'd lost but had been good losers. They'd showed genuine interest in her research, unlike the people in our town.

"I haven't seen you since uni. Except when my parents shove another Emily article in my face." He laughed heartily.

I stepped closer to Emily.

She grinned. "Ah, the two person Emily Fan Club."

"Yeah. I'm pretty sure they're devastated you knocked me back that one time I dared to ask you out at uni."

What? I took another step closer to Emily. We were only an inch or two apart. Callum glanced at me; his mouth lifted at one side. I clenched my teeth harder. I kept silent; this wasn't my conversation.

"How's it feel to be back in the one place you vowed never to return to?"

I sucked my breath in. Hearing those words again were like a sucker punch.

WE SAT on the back tray of my ute, our legs dangling over the edge, looking out over the fields. When she rested her hand on her thigh it touched mine, sending sparks of electricity through me.

My hand inched towards hers. I pulled it back. There was no point. Emily didn't love me the way I loved her.

"I'm not coming back, Luke. When I leave for uni, I'm leaving all this behind."

My chest constricted. Words wouldn't come.

Emily turned to me. "I'll miss you. I'll miss this. Us."

But not enough to want to stay with me. Or return to me. There wasn't even a fleeting moment in her mind where she doubted her future. I doubted mine all the time. A future without Emily was like a future where the sun's rays were muted.

"I'M LIVING proof that you should never say never," Emily said.

"Yeah, I can see that."

"Nothing's changed. The town still hates me."

I bit my lip and looked down at my feet. How could I ever expect her to stay? It was beyond selfish. Her fingers were flexing at her side. I took hold of her hand and gave it a squeeze. Emily turned to me and I swore I saw something in her eyes I'd never seen before. Love. Realisation. Awakening. I couldn't name it, but it was radiating from her. My heart rate quickened.

"Right. Nothing's changed," Callum said.

No, nothing. Except I had the tiniest spark of hope. When I faced him, he was smirking. He took the bag and scanned it.

"Are you just visiting?"

"My dad's sick. I came back to care for him."

He reached across the counter and took Emily's other hand. I couldn't stop staring at their hands as his lingered. "I'm sorry to hear that."

"Thanks. I'll be here until the time comes for me to put the farm on the market."

"Shit." He still had her hand. I wanted to reach over and push his away or crush it in mine, either would do.

"How much do we owe you?" I asked, pulling my wallet out.

Emily withdrew her hand from Callum and picked up the bag of food.

"Thirteen dollars."

I handed my card over, eager to get out of there before they had another *moment*.

"You should come out. Check out the farm. It might be a good fit for your plans," Emily said, almost cheerful.

"Yeah. OK. How about next Saturday?"

"Great."

Emily almost bounced out the door. She'd never, in twenty-five years, bounced for me.

"It would be terrific if Callum bought the farm because he

believes in sustainability and would work with the land so it would be ideal," Emily rambled.

"Yeah. Ideal."

"It would be the best solution. I can't wait for next Saturday."

I could.

CHAPTER FIFTEEN

Emily

Aɪsʜᴀ ᴀɴᴅ Dᴀʟɪʀ Sʜᴀʀɪꜰ sat on the porch with Dad and Luke while I went inside to make tea. Luke had been strange all morning. It was weird. Up until our visit to Brodsky's he'd been fine. His normal Luke self. He seemed to change after he'd held my hand. Maybe he'd read my thoughts when I'd looked at him. He'd always known what I was thinking, sometimes before I did and at that moment, in that store, in front of Callum, I'd thought about kissing him.

I was so stupid. Luke had never shown any interest in me other than being friends even though he was always there for me. Always. I enjoyed spending time with him more than anyone else in the world. Had he read my mind and freaked out?

Filling the kettle, I shook my head. I kept busy, getting the cups out of the overhead cupboard while I waited for the kettle to boil. My thoughts strayed to Luke's lips, his strong arms, his hands—so much bigger than mine but so gentle, roaming across my body. I dragged my thoughts away. There was no point ruining our friendship for a kiss.

The kitchen door creaked as it opened. Luke came in, running his hand through his hair. He was nervous. What had I done? One stupid slip had led to this. Not even a kiss. A dream of a kiss.

"Need a hand?" he asked, coming over to where the cups were sitting.

"My saviour," I said, giving him a hip bump. I wanted the old Luke back. I handed him the plate of Tim Tams and started pouring the cups of tea. He grabbed one and took it outside. I watched him leaving, longer than I should have, but damn his arse filled his shorts nicely. Dragging my eyes away from him, I picked up the other two cups and headed out.

Luke met me at the door.

"There's a jug of water for us on the sink," I said to him.

I placed the cups on the table in front of Aisha and Dalir. Dalir was holding Shorty. He brought the rabbit close to his face and nuzzled him. "He is just beautiful."

Dad's smile was broad, like a proud parent. "He is such a good boy. He drinks and eats more and more every day."

I sat next to Dad. He'd become more tired over the past two weeks, sleeping more, and eating less. I tried to make sure what he did eat was nutrient rich. Except the Tim Tams which were his favourite, and he ate at least once a day. "Dad feeds him every three hours, except at night time."

"He sleeps through the night. The only other baby who did that was Emmaline."

I sucked in my breath. Dad never used that name. He

didn't appear to notice what he'd said. My childhood before the accident was never spoken of, almost as if it didn't exist.

"Emily was the best baby in the house. She was the best child, too. She was always helpful."

I'd tried to help as much as I could, whether it was Mum or Dad. When I'd helped, it was my alone time with them. Time I didn't need to share with my brothers or sister. That's what I'd been doing the day of the accident.

MUM DROVE the quad while I knelt on the seat behind her. It was the only way I could see where we were going. We sang Waltzing Matilda at the top of our lungs. We weren't going fast but my long hair still whipped around my face.

The track was bumpy, and I bounced as the wheels moved over the uneven ground. I held tight to Mum's shoulders as we made a turn. Turns were my favourite. Even though we were going slow I still swayed from side to side. Mum's body stayed rigid, helping me balance. I laughed as we continued our ride.

We stopped at the water pump shed—three wooden sides and a tin roof. Mum went to the river and closed the water inlet while I turned the power off. We needed to investigate the lack of water through the irrigation system. First step, checking the pump. As Mum worked, I handed her the tools like a surgical nurse would hand the doctor scalpels and clamps.

"OK Emily, go and switch the power back on."

I made my way around the back of the shed. My feet sinking in the green grass and mud. Mum said the pump must have been leaking for a while to make such a mess. I reached the power box, standing on tip toes, my cold toes sinking into the wet earth.

"Is it OK to turn on now, Mum?"

"Yes. Go ahead."

I flicked the switch and waited in the silence. Nothing happened.

"OK. We need to go down to the river now," Mum called out.

We descended the metal stairs to the river to turn the lever on for the water. My little hands wrapped around the lever. Mum's hands were over mine as we pulled it towards us. We stood and listened as the water rushed into the pipe.

"It's funny how it whooshed in and then stopped so suddenly, don't you think?" Mum asked.

"Yes. Like when we play Mr Wolf. We all run and as soon as he turns around, we stop on the spot."

"You're good at that game," Mum said, smoothing down my hair.

"Everyone looks at the wolf's body, but I watch the head. The wolf is listening so hard that he turns his head first."

"You're so smart, Emmaline. You are going to make a difference in this world."

I hugged her around her waist. Mum's warm arms circled me and she bent to kiss the top of my head.

"Let's go," she said, pulling away.

I followed her up the stairs, staring down at my feet and the grass growing through the metal grating. I kept looking, trying to find an orchid. Mum and I had spotted them there before, white and purple flowers amongst all the green. I held tightly to the railing for balance.

Mum yelled out. My eyes darted to her. Wasps buzzed around her and she shook her hand. It banged against the rail-

ing, her ring clicking against it, metal against metal. As she waved her other hand above her head, her body twisted. She fell towards me. Her hands grabbed at the railing but missed. She crashed into me.

"Emmaline," she called out as we fell, our bodies entwined, smashing into step after step.

"EMILY?"

I shook the memory away and glanced around the table. Who'd spoken to me? I couldn't tell because every pair of eyes peered at me.

"Sorry. I missed that."

Aisha spoke. "Did you have any pets growing up?"

"No. I wasn't allowed."

Dalir handed Shorty to Aisha.

"Here, you can feed him," Dad said, handing the syringe over.

Aisha beamed. She held Shorty ever so gently and raised the syringe to his lips.

"Just press the plunger slowly. He will tell you when he's had enough by shaking his head."

"We had a cat when I was a child," Dalir said. "It was just an ordinary alley cat we found when he was young."

Dad looked over at me. "Emily wanted a kitten once." He gave me a small smile. "I said no. I didn't want her to have any reason to stay here."

Aisha and Dalir turned their attention to Shorty. Luke watched me as I stared dumbfounded at Dad. He'd wanted me to leave so badly that he didn't want me to have a pet? Was this some kind of new cruelty? I swallowed the lump in my throat.

"Will you keep Shorty when he's grown?" Aisha asked breaking the silence.

"No," Dad said. "You're not allowed to keep rabbits in Queensland."

"Oh, that's a shame. He is delightful."

After Aisha and Dalir left, Luke and I washed the dishes while Dad went for his nap. I couldn't stop thinking about Dad's revelation. How could you love your child so little that you made sure you did everything in your power to make sure they left?

"That was a big thing for your dad to admit," Luke said as he took a glass from me.

"What? To tell your child you didn't want them?"

I couldn't look at Luke, scared my face would betray me, or the tears clouding my vision would fall.

"That's not what he said."

"That's exactly what he said."

Luke put the tea towel and glass down on the bench. He took my shoulders and turned me towards him. I bit my tongue, holding my tears back.

"Emily, that's not what he meant. He didn't want you to stay because he hated this town and how they treated you. He loved you so much that he wanted you to be free."

I couldn't comprehend what he was saying. Dad pushed me away all of my life because he loved me? Would you do that to someone you loved? I tried to read Luke's expression. He raised his hand to my face and cupped my cheek. The warmth, the steadiness fought against my racing thoughts to calm me.

"No. He meant he didn't want me here. He's never wanted me here." Saying the truth out loud after keeping it in all these years was hard. The tears threatened to fall.

"He didn't want you to be tied to this place. He even waited until you left before he started putting your ideas into action because he didn't want you to be so excited you stayed. He didn't want you to have a kitten because he didn't want you to be attached…"

I shook my head. It didn't make sense; what Luke was saying made no sense.

"He loved you *so much* he withheld himself from you."

All this time I'd thought the opposite. This was too unreal. How could all my beliefs be washed away after all these years? Luke put his arms around me and pulled me in close. I held onto him like my body was about to float away and he was the only thing keeping me grounded. Luke always kept me grounded, kept me out of trouble, made me feel loved. Luke was my everything.

And Luke would never lie to me. He would never tell me Dad loved me if it weren't true.

I took a deep breath and pulled away. Heat rushed through me as Luke held eye contact with me. I took my bottom lip between my teeth. Luke's gaze dropped to my lips. I wanted him to kiss me, and I didn't care if he knew. Even though I stood stock still I could feel my body moving towards him, like when you were on a roller coaster and you had no control over the velocity. He moved closer. His breath warmed my skin as he bent his head to mine. I breathed him in, and goosebumps erupted on my skin.

Luke was close. So close, that even when he paused millimetres from my lips, I could feel his, like the air between us was caressing us, linking us. My lips opened to his as soon as his soft mouth met mine. Wrapping my arms around him, I pulled him closer. The warmth of his mouth, the stroke of his tongue, the sweet trace of Tim Tams—it was more than I ever dreamed of.

CHAPTER SIXTEEN

Luke

"What is with you tonight?" Mum asked as she led us to our chairs at the back of the hall.

"What?"

"You've been acting weird all afternoon. I'm sure you're not even listening to me half the time."

"Just thinking."

"About Emily?"

"About lots of things."

Truth was all I could think about was Emily and that kiss. I'd dreamt about kissing her for years. Always wondering if her lips were as soft as they looked. They were. If I closed my eyes, I could feel her body pressed against mine and her tongue as it danced with mine. I played the kiss over and over in my mind. Had she enjoyed it as much as I had?

After the kiss had finished, I'd pulled away and stared at her, heat rising in my cheeks. I wanted to kiss her again, but the silence and staring stretched out until it got to the point that I couldn't stand there anymore. Declaring I had to go to the farmers co-op meeting, I made my way to the door. My hand paused before pulling on the handle. What was I doing? Why was I leaving? I turned back to Emily. She hadn't moved. She was still standing there staring at me. I opened the door and left.

And now all I could think of was that kiss. It was like some kind of black hole that kept dragging me in, making time slow. Like her short brown hair and intense green eyes, that kiss was a beautiful, perfect snare.

Mum smiled that ever-knowing mum smile.

I turned my attention to the people standing in small groups. I didn't want Mum to know what I was thinking about. I didn't even know what I was thinking about half the time. Not since Emily had returned. The groups in front of me were cliques that had existed since high school—my parents' generation and mine. No one ever looked happy. Not truly happy. Is that what they were like at home? I couldn't imagine sitting around the dinner table not smiling or laughing. My home was the opposite. We enjoyed each other's company. We worked together as a team. We laughed. We had fun. Even though I was a fully grown adult it wasn't strange to me to be so close to my parents.

"I hate coming here," Mum said. "Jim was right to stop coming years ago."

I nodded. If it wasn't for the special speaker they had scheduled, I wouldn't have come, but the manager from Sunshine Water was someone we should listen to. He would be talking about current water levels, rainfall predictions and what that would mean for us farmers in the next water allocation.

"It's going to be strange without Jim next door. Especially for your Dad, they've been neighbours since they were born."

And him being gone would mean Emily had no reason to return.

Footsteps approached. Bianca stopped in the aisle beside me. She had a full face of make up on, skin-tight jeans and a shirt with buttons open to show plenty of cleavage. Only Queen B would get dressed up for a farmer's meeting. She could wear as much make up as she liked, I still wouldn't be attracted to her.

She rested her hand on my shoulder and bent down so I could get a full view. She was just like her mother. I looked away. "I can't thank you enough for what you're doing for the community."

I wanted to move but was afraid if I sat back in my chair she'd end up in my lap. She stood and turned back to face the room. When she caught her mother's eye, she nodded.

Mrs Phillips called out, "OK. Let's get this meeting started."

Everyone took their seats and turned their attention to Mrs Phillips.

"Last time we met, we sent Luke on a recon mission. We asked him to learn what Emily Watson is doing here."

She looked directly at me. The farmers did the same. Bianca rubbed my shoulder. I stiffened. Why couldn't she just leave me alone? Why couldn't they leave Emily alone?

Bianca smiled down at me and spoke. "Luke hasn't only spent time with Emily sourcing information from her. He's been seen out with her. Word on the street is that he's dating her."

What the hell? Bianca rubbed my shoulder again before

her fingers caressed my neck. I cringed. I moved towards Mum hoping Bianca's hand would fall away. It didn't.

I would like nothing better than dating Emily. Well, that was a lie. There were a few things I'd like better.

"I—"

"Thank you, Luke," Mrs Phillips said, beaming at me. "You've gone beyond the call of duty."

"That's right. No one would date Emily unless they had an ulterior motive," Bianca chimed in. "I mean, seriously, no one is that desperate. She's pathetic."

Laughter. I shrugged my shoulders removing Bianca's hand. Desperate? Bianca was the one who was desperate. Always chasing after me when she knew the only person I wanted was Emily.

"No—"

"We'll wait for your report at the next meeting," Mrs Phillips said before continuing the meeting. Bianca moved away.

"What the fuck is wrong with you?" Mum angry whispered at me.

"What?"

"Do you really want to go down that rabbit hole?"

I shook my head confused.

"Pretending to date Emily because she's desperate." Mum's mouth was a tight line.

Resting my elbows on my knees, I glared at the floor between my feet. What the fuck *was* wrong with me? I couldn't believe I'd just sat there and let them say those things about Emily. I let them all insult her.

This was bad. So bad. First the spying and now this. How

could I do this to Emily? Even worse how could I let *them* do this to Emily?

Unclenching my jaw, I sat up. I wouldn't allow them to treat Emily this way. Just as I was ready to open my mouth, Mrs Phillips said, "Let's welcome tonight's guest speaker…"

CHAPTER SEVENTEEN

Emily

"The talk starts at six-thirty," I said to Dad as he fed Shorty.

He'd asked me to cut some grass so Shorty had something different to eat. When I brought it in Dad laughed. He indicated to Shorty. "He's a bit small to be eating that much."

The amount of grass I held was extreme. It would take him a week to eat it all. I laughed, too.

"What are you going to talk about?"

"They've asked me to talk about farms that have been transformed."

"Farms that you've transformed?" Dad asked, raising his eyes to mine.

"I thought I'd talk about one that's not mine and one I've helped with."

"Is Luke coming?"

Luke who'd kissed me the day before. I blushed just thinking about it. The blush was nothing compared to how hot that kiss made me feel. Another thing to add to that perfect boyfriend list.

Luke had kissed me. He'd made the first move. Surely that meant he really wanted to do it. It wasn't just a spur of the moment thing. A mistake. The way he'd left, without saying a word, had me wondering if he'd even meant it at all. I realised Dad was looking at me waiting for an answer.

"Yes, he said he'd pick us up at five-thirty."

Dad put Shorty down in his plastic box so he could eat some grass. I checked his litter tray. It was in the corner of the box where he liked to toilet. We used paper litter in case Shorty decided to eat it, which the toilet training videos said he might do. He had plenty of hay waiting for him in the tray. Who would have thought that rabbits liked to eat and poop at the same time? Then again, who would have thought rabbits could be toilet trained?

"I guess Shorty will be OK," he said.

"I think he can survive without you for a few hours. Can you survive without him?"

"I'll just have to force myself," he said, giving me a smile. "I haven't listened to you give a talk since high school."

My stomach did a small lurch. He was excited to hear me speak. I still found it hard to believe what Luke said—that Dad loved me.

LUKE, Dad, and I walked into the hall. It was full of chatter and laughter. People were nodding and smiling while they spoke to each other. We stood off to the side, glancing around. Susie, Bruce, and Callum were at the front of the room.

Callum noticed us first and gave us a wave. Susie came over. She may have been short but her energy burst through, like even the room had trouble containing her.

"We've saved you some seats at the front," she said.

She led us there as everyone watched us. Their faces were friendly and open. The tension left my muscles and I smiled at those watching us. I felt welcome here, unlike my own hometown. Callum took a seat next to me with Dad on the other side and Luke beside him. Dad and Luke said something to each other. Luke's jaw was set. He kept his eyes forward. I took my laptop out of my bag, my hands shaking.

Susie made her way to the microphone. The crowd found their seats and the hall became quiet.

"Good evening. Thank you all for joining us tonight. I know you're all excited to hear from our guest speaker. Let's welcome Emily Watson."

Dad patted my leg before I stood up. Applause sounded around the room. Susie took my laptop and plugged it in so I could start the slide show.

"Thank you all for having me here tonight. Susie told me you all took a vote and you've chosen for me to speak about farm transformations."

Eager faces peered at me, nodding. Dad and Luke looked around, too. When they faced me again, they both smiled. Peace settled over me as I smiled back at the two most important people in my life.

"I'm going to talk about two inspirational stories—Banrock Station in South Australia and a farm I worked with in Victoria. I welcome questions at any time. Just raise your hand to grab my attention."

I opened the slide show. The pictures rotated slowly, allowing everyone to have a good look.

"Banrock Station is in South Australia. Some of you may know it for its wines. It wasn't always a winery. 40,000 years ago, Aboriginals lived there. We know this from scar trees and other sacred sites found in the area. We also know from years of studies that Aboriginals worked with the land and not against it. They did farm, but on a much smaller scale than has occurred since European settlement. In 1851 the land was developed for pastoral grazing."

Old photos, faded black and white with muted lighting, appeared on the screen showing sheep and cattle, the land overgrazed and then cleared for crop production. It was dry and sparse.

"In the 1920s locks installed along the Murray River increased flooding to the area. The European carp invaded, river red gums died, and salinity increased."

The faces around the room reflected my feelings about the devastation. It was sad to see the land raped and pillaged. Trees, once tall and majestic, stood dead in the water. The room was quiet, the mood sombre. Anticipation flooded through me at the knowledge of what I was about to share with them all.

"In 1992 that all changed. Sheep were removed. Landowners Bruce and Teri Engel worked with other organisations to restore the wetlands. They installed flow control structures. This allowed for a natural cycle of drying and filling of the wetlands."

New photos showed the abundance of flora and fauna. There were boardwalks framed by tall native grasses and juvenile gum trees. Dead trees with their bare trunks were surrounded by reeds and lilies filled ponds. Birds and more birds. Water and trees. Green everywhere.

"Ten years later Banrock Station was listed under the Ramsar Convention as a Wetland of International Importance."

The photos scrolled on.

"The vineyard is hugely successful. They use a computerised irrigation system. Moisture is measured every thirty minutes and water is delivered through drippers below the surface."

Callum raised his hand. I nodded at him. "What's the benefit of this system?"

"It's estimated that water usage is reduced by 20% because water is delivered below the surface and evaporation is reduced."

Murmurs around the room. This technology wouldn't be suitable with their current crops because of the ploughing but it could be if they changed their crops or farming practices.

"This isn't the only water saving technique they use," I said, bringing their attention back to me. "Mulch is also part of their strategy. Many farms could incorporate this. My father and Luke have implemented the use of cover crops to suppress weeds and return nutrients to the soil once cut and used as mulch."

"Does the wet/dry cycle save water too?" Callum asked. I smiled at him. He knew all the right questions to ask.

"1.15 gigalitres over a two-year cycle."

Eyes widened and mouths fell open. I didn't need to explain to them that 1.15 gigalitres equalled 1150 Olympic sized swimming pools. They were farmers. They knew measurements of water like their life depended on it. Well, their crop's life, and in turn theirs.

They nodded appreciatively. I glanced at Dad and Luke who were pointing at the screen and speaking quietly to each other, like some of the other farmers were doing.

"The next place I want to talk about is one I assisted on in Victoria, while I was still at uni. Has anyone heard of Poppy Dene?"

I looked around the room for acknowledgement. Luke nodded. He knew the story. I'd shared every step of it with him. When my eyes fell on Callum, he raised his hand. Luke glanced at Callum and frowned. I shrugged it off and continued.

"Right, I see a couple of you know about Poppy Dene. Let me share it with the rest of you."

I started the slide show depicting a barren land. It was like many farms across Australia—cleared, overgrazed, desolate. The farmers were silent.

"Here's a random fact for you. Did you know that since European settlement forty-four percent of Australian forests and woodlands have been cleared? And land clearing is the biggest driver of animal extinction?"

Heads shook.

"This is what land clearing looks like." I pointed to the photos of Poppy Dene—brown, dry, depressing. "The reasoning behind it is simple. The more land cleared the more land that can be farmed. But cleared land does not mean fertile land."

Some of the farmers nodded. We all knew how we added fertiliser to the soil every year for a more successful crop. The crops were what brought in money and most would do anything they could to improve them. However, being a farmer in Australia was more than just manipulating the land for personal benefit. Many modern farmers recognised that. They nurtured the land. They wanted the best for it and themselves. Some just needed help to find the balance. I was proud of being a farmer's daughter and helping farmers find that balance.

"When the current owner of Poppy Dene took over the farm, nothing changed...at first. They overstocked and used chemicals. And why not? It was normal practice. One day they came to the conclusion that it had to change."

The slides then showed a barren, naked landscape next to a green fertile scene. Cleared land next to land planted with trees. A dry landscape beside wetlands.

"How did they get from that to that?" a farmer asked looking from left to right.

I was encouraged by his question. "They started with planting trees and shrubs. Lots of them."

"What sort of trees?"

"Indigenous and foreign. They started with pines as a windbreak to shelter their sheep. They were happy with their progress but were unsure if that's what they should continue doing. That's when they put a call out, that I answered. I got a group together and we went down during our summer holidays."

I remembered how we'd learnt so much together and they were always open to ideas. They'd listened and learned while we did the same. We didn't just learn about flora and fauna; we'd learnt about working with farmers and their constraints.

"We investigated what trees grew indigenously in the area, using historical photos and going to local state and national parks, areas that weren't cleared. We visited nurseries to see what they stocked. We wanted indigenous trees because they were suited to the local conditions and had a symbiotic relationship with soil fungi. We planted understory plants as well. Indigenous trees are also important to the local wildlife. You may wonder why that's important, and I'll get to that."

"So, you recreated the local environment," Callum said.

I nodded.

"But all that green didn't come from planting trees alone," a farmer said, pointing at the photos and the ground cover.

"You're right. The trees brought birds and the birds ate insects, so insecticides weren't needed in large quantities. They reduced stock levels. There was no way the land could sustain the current levels going forward. With the amount of inputs needed to keep those stock levels it was actually a negative return. After that, we decided to stop using superphosphates due to the damage they can cause the environment. Slowly, natural grasses returned."

The room took a collective breath. I glanced around at the farmers. Unlike Alma, these farmers were interested in what I had to say. They didn't say it was preposterous to get rid of superphosphates, something farmers relied on. These farmers were progressive rather than conservative. They knew the way things were done needed to change, for both their farms and the environment. I glanced around the room trying to spot farmers who wanted to ask questions.

I caught Dad's eye. He looked at me with pride, something so rare it made my heart lift. Luke had the same expression. And he was the one who made all of this possible. He believed in me so much that I believed in myself. He'd always listened to me, asked questions, encouraged me. He never tired of my conversations.

"What about all the water?" another farmer asked, pointing to the wetlands displayed on the screen.

I smiled at him. "When the land was cleared all those years ago, they'd drained the wetlands as well. You know, the more land for farming thing. So, they plugged up the drains and the wetlands started to fill naturally. Again, birds and other fauna became abundant. The more birds and bees the more pollination, more growth."

I let the slideshow play out. The farmers eyes drifted from the screen to me, not one uttered a word.

"That's all we have time for today. I know as farmers we always need to be aware of balance. Balance of producing food for our community, producing a viable income while maintaining a fertile farm as well as being stewards for the environment. It's a lot to keep in harmony. The examples I've given you are large scale examples. They cost money. Money most farmers don't have. You can start small, make small changes. Also, don't forget there are a range of grants available, too."

"How does your business help farmers?" Callum asked.

Sweat coated my skin. I wasn't here to give a sales pitch. I just wanted to share my passion with a willing audience. I had multiple income streams. I talked at conferences about farming sustainably and how farmers could improve their farming practices. I was always open and transparent about the commission I stood to receive when I recommended equipment to farmers. If it wasn't right or they weren't ready, I wouldn't recommend anything. I wrote articles for different publications. Then there was my consulting arm where I worked with farmers to improve sustainability and helped them change their farming practices if required. That was the best part. All the rest paid the bills, but the farmers are what made it all worthwhile.

"I work with farmers to see where improvements can be made on their farms. We look at different avenues, whether small or large, and work on a plan together. Sometimes it's not the right time for the farmers to implement the plans. If that's the case, they can always contact me when they are ready, and we can re-evaluate."

"Does that happen often?"

"Not really, farmers are usually ready to start implementing something by the time they contact me. They just need a little guidance."

Callum and other farmers nodded. I sighed, grateful that part was over.

Susie came to stand beside me. "Thanks Emily, for sharing your wisdom with us."

A round of applause sounded. I blushed, not knowing where to look. Callum was clapping and smiling broadly. I stepped away and made my way back to my seat. Before I could sit, a farmer approached and asked me a question. Callum joined him. I appreciated his support, but I found myself looking for Luke. He was the one I wanted by my side to share everything with. When I was awarded a new contract or finished a job, he was always the first one I called. I wanted him to come over so I could hold his hand. I wanted him to be a part of this, like he was a part of everything else.

When I finally made eye contact with Luke, I hoped he'd read the invitation on my face, but he stayed seated with Dad. Callum put his hand on the small of my back and led me around the room. He was so cheerful with the other farmers that when he laughed and joked, I couldn't help but join in. I was grateful to him for helping me feel relaxed.

I glanced back at Luke. All he did was give me a small smile. What was going on with him? He'd been weird since the kiss. Did he think it was a mistake?

CHAPTER EIGHTEEN

Luke

CALLUM WALKED up the driveway and Emily went out to meet him. I raised my hand in greeting but stayed on the porch with Jim. I didn't need to be in the Emily/Callum bubble. So, I stood at the railing, watching them like a creeper. As they set off Callum put his hand on the small of her back just like he'd done last week at the meeting. Touching Emily seemed so natural to him. Even when he let go, they stayed close. They walked to the end of the field looking back once. Callum said something and Emily laughed, turning her attention back to him.

I could tell she liked being with him by the way she walked with so much energy. I could feel it from where I stood. She turned into him when he spoke, gazing up into his face. My hands hurt from clutching the railing too tight. I kicked at the post, visualising Callum's shin.

"Looks like you left your run eight years too late," Jim said from behind me.

I clenched my jaw. I should have known better than to get my hopes up. The kiss the other day meant nothing. Just a moment in time never to be repeated. It's what I deserved for not putting up an argument about the fake dating and then for not telling Emily about it. I was too ashamed. Not just about the fake dating, but for what I'd allowed them to say. Dad would have never stood for something like that if they were talking about Mum.

"I'm going to work on the tractor," I said, turning away from the retreating couple. I swear when I glanced at Jim there was a hint of a smile. He was lucky I didn't kick him in the shin.

I stalked down the stairs and across the yard to the shed. It was better that I kept myself busy rather than watch Emily and Callum. Just the thought of them had my muscles tensing. Grabbing a spanner and the draining bucket I made my way to the tractor. I lay on the ground and manoeuvred myself underneath it so I could reach the drain plugs easily and undid them. The oil came gushing out of each hole in a stream and I watched until each stream slowed to drips. The oil was clean, a light brown with a hint of amber. For anyone who didn't know Jim, it would be obvious from the oil alone that he maintained his equipment well. I put the plugs back in and tightened them, then took my rag and cleaned around the plugs to remove any dirt.

After moving out from under the tractor, I stood up and peered out into the field. I couldn't see them. Perhaps they were at the pumphouse. Emily had been scared to go back there after the accident. We hadn't gone near it for months after she'd gotten out of the hospital...until one day she'd asked me to go with her.

. . .

EMILY and I were crossing the field to go to my house for lunch.

"I want to go to the pumphouse," she said.

"OK."

I took her hand and led her off the path, crossing the rows of vegetables. I expected her to stop at the pumphouse and slowed my steps when we neared it. She kept going though and approached the stairs. When we got close her steps faltered. I held onto her little hand tighter. It trembled in mine. Even though her steps slowed she didn't stop walking, not until we reached the top of the stairs.

We'd stood there together, looking down at the metal steps. Chills ran through me, remembering the blood I saw there after the accident. My parents told me Emily's mum had broken her neck. They were found at the bottom, Emily wrapped in her arms. Jim thought they were both dead.

I didn't dare let go of her hand; for me or for her. Emily had reached out her other hand and ran it across the railing. I planted my feet firm, just in case, scared that we might fall even though the fear was unrealistic.

Tears ran down her cheeks. If I hadn't looked at her, I wouldn't have known she was crying. I don't know how long we stood like that for. I don't know if she was remembering what happened or if she was having a conversation with her mum. She hadn't spoken a word. When she was ready, she'd turned away and I followed.

. . .

I WOULD FOLLOW her anywhere but not when she left for university. Why hadn't I followed her then? Did I not love her enough? Maybe what Mum said was true. It didn't matter. It was done now. I shook my head and returned my attention to the task at hand.

Scanning the tool board above the bench, I spotted the filter wrench. After grabbing it I made my way back to the tractor to remove the oil filter. It was heavy, full of oil and I drained it into the bucket. I checked the filter gasket to make sure it wasn't torn and then ran my finger around the plate on the engine block to make sure there was no gasket residue there. Satisfied it was clean I grabbed the new filter. I coated the new gasket with a few drops of oil to lubricate it. Dad told me it helped seal it better.

I screwed the new filter on and tightened it until it made solid contact. I gave it another quarter turn. It would be tight but not too tight.

As I stepped back, footsteps sounded behind me. Not Emily's footsteps. These were heavier. I stiffened.

"Emily tells me that you've been planting some trees to block the wind and reduce soil erosion," Callum said.

"That's right."

"She said I should ask you about the soil condition seeing as she hasn't been here for a while."

I sighed inwardly. No, she hadn't been here for a while and she'd be gone again soon. Maybe even to his town, with his perfect farmers. Did she want me to tell him it's great so he'd buy the farm? Then I'd have to be faced with the Emily/Callum bubble for the rest of my life. Would she stay for Callum? My brain was no longer having coherent thoughts. All I could see was them walking off together, smiling and laughing.

I turned to Callum. He was open, friendly, just like he'd always been. I needed to grow up. It wasn't his fault I'd lost my chance with Emily.

"We've been working over the past few years to improve the condition. The trees we've planted have increased the fertility of the surrounding soil by creating organic matter."

He nodded, walking around the shed checking out the equipment. "Why aren't you buying the farm?"

"She didn't ask me."

His head snapped towards me. "Really? I thought you would be the first person she would ask. You've always been as thick as thieves."

"I guess things change." I didn't want to have this conversation with him. I didn't even want to have it with myself.

He shook his head. "Not from what I see."

"What?" I narrowed my eyes at him.

"Come on, Luke. You two are in love with each other as much today as you were eight, ten, twelve years ago."

"What are you talking about?"

He looked at me like I was all kinds of stupid. "Are you serious?"

I stared at him.

"Last week at the talk you couldn't keep your eyes off each other."

"From what I recall her attention was on you mostly."

"She is not remotely interested in me. Remember how I said I asked her out once at uni?"

How could I forget?

"I needn't have bothered. No one could compare to you."

"Huh?"

He raised his eyebrows.

"It was always Luke this and Luke that and heaven forbid if we asked her to do anything on a 'I'm calling Luke tonight' night."

We'd never missed a phone call. That didn't mean she was in love with me, though.

"And what about that day you came into the store? At the slightest sign she was upset you were right there, holding her hand."

"That's what friends do."

He gave me an exasperated smile. "God, you're dense."

I peered at him closely.

He smiled and shook his head. "Seriously, do friends look at each other with adoration written all over their face...since they were twelve?"

He rolled his eyes as I just stared at him.

"I think I'll put an offer on the farm. OK with you?"

I nodded. That's all I could manage.

"Good."

I watched him walk out.

I was putting the oil back in the cupboard as Emily walked into the shed. I leant back on the bench, not sure what to do. Was what Callum said really true? Was Emily in love with me? If it was true, no, even if it wasn't, I needed to tell her about the farmers co-op. She deserved to know. My dreams and guilt were rolling around in my stomach like acrobats doing somersaults in molasses.

"What's wrong?" Emily asked, her pace picking up.

"Nothing."

She stopped in front of me. "Are you sure?"

I could be sure. I could reach out, pull her towards me, kiss her. She'd accepted me the other day. If she loved me, she would accept me again.

She shook her head and shrugged. "Callum has put an offer on the farm."

I nodded.

"He said you wanted to talk to me. Is that what you wanted to talk about?"

Talking wasn't on my agenda. Fuck it, what was I even waiting for? I took a step towards her and pushed my guilt to the nether regions of my mind.

"I don't want to talk."

My eyes dropped to her lips. Her soft, inviting lips. The somersaults turned into tumble turns. Whack, whack, whack, against my insides.

"Luke—"

My lips cut off her words. My hand cupped the back of her head, my fingers entwined in her short brown hair. She tensed then relaxed all in a split second. Her lips opened to mine. Wrapping my arms around her, I pulled her towards me. She still wasn't close enough. I reached down, grabbed her arse, and lifted her. Her legs encircled me in an instant. I kissed her like a madman letting out ten years of repressed feelings.

I pushed her against the front wheel of the tractor so she could half sit on it and my hands could wander. I ran them up her thighs, my thumbs on the inside stopping just at the junction. Her breathing faltered. We needed to be closer. I needed her to feel how much I wanted her. I tilted my hips so Emily could feel my hardness pressed against her.

I pulled away. My words escaped on a breathy sigh. "I love you."

Her response was to pull me closer, to kiss me harder.

CHAPTER NINETEEN

Emily

"You're not eating dinner with me?" Dad asked as I set his plate before him and sat down in my chair.

"No. Luke is picking me up in a few minutes."

"Right. Because you two don't already spend enough time together." He spooned some mashed potato into his mouth and raised his eyebrows at me.

"I don't know what you're talking about."

"Sure, you don't. It's two weeks since Callum threatened to move in on you, and you two have barely been apart." Another spoonful, as if it were an exclamation mark.

"Callum did no such thing."

"That's not what Luke thought." This spoonful came with a smile.

I cocked my head, suspicious as hell. "Dad, what did you do?"

"I didn't do anything. You're the one who walked off with Callum, smiling and laughing, leaving Luke behind."

I thought back. That's not what happened. Well, not in the way he'd insinuated. How would I have felt if that were Luke and Bianca? I shook my head. That was nowhere near the same thing. Bianca is a bitch; Callum is a nice guy.

"Hmph," Dad grunted as he took another mouthful.

"Just eat your mash." I rolled my eyes at him.

My heart felt full for the first time since the accident. Every day, not only did Luke and I get closer, but so did Dad and I. He was a different man than the one I'd left behind, the one I'd known most of my life. The one who was sullen and quiet. Who I thought only attended school events or sports events because it was a parental requirement, not because he wanted to. The one who dismissed me without warning, who didn't hug me or comfort me.

Instead, he was open. He talked to me not because he had to but because he wanted to. He laughed. His words were kind, not that they'd ever been mean. If I thought back, he'd always been there to support me when it was needed—his hand on my side at the fateful meeting and the ruffling of my air at the football. He turned up to every parent teacher night unlike most parents. He supported me while the rest of the town turned on me. All of it was more evident to me now that I'd put my hurt aside, that I wasn't guarding my heart with every breath.

Shorty hopped around the kitchen. He stopped under Dad's chair and lifted his tail. I made for him but was too slow. A small puddle of liquid appeared near Dad's foot. I shook my head.

"Apparently Shorty thinks you're his territory."

Dad looked under his chair and laughed.

I grabbed some paper towel and wiped the liquid up.

Then I took the culprit and the paper towel and placed them both in the litter box.

As I washed my hands, Luke's car lights lit up the window while he parked in the driveway. They turned off and moments later his car door opened and closed. I went to the table and grabbed my bag. I had no idea where we were going. He'd said I didn't need to dress up, so jeans, t-shirt and flats it was.

As the screen door opened, I smiled. Not just at the sight of Luke but because he was so comfortable here that he didn't even knock.

"Hi, Jim."

"Luke." He indicated to his lonely bowl. "I'm not too happy about having to eat alone."

"You'll live."

"No, actually, I won't."

Luke's face paled. Wide eyed I turned to Dad as he licked his spoon. I couldn't believe he was using his imminent death to tease Luke. "That's not funny."

Dad gave a small shrug. "I know. You're right, but the look on Luke's face was priceless."

I glared at him.

"You're such an arse," Luke said, shaking his head.

"I do my best."

Luke ignored him and turned to me instead. "Ready?"

"Sure am. Where are we going?"

"You'll see."

"Twenty-five years, and finally your first date," Dad called after us.

Our first date. That made me feel both excited and nervous. What did Luke have planned?

"This isn't really our first date," Luke said.

I looked at him sideways as we hopped into the car.

"Remember when I got my licence? You were the first one I took for a drive."

I narrowed my eyes at him. "That wasn't a date."

"No, but I wanted it to be."

LUKE SMILED BROADLY as we drove the open roads. His window was down, and the wind tousled his already messy hair. I had one foot tucked under me and the other up on the dash, singing along to a song on the radio. I'd never sing in front of anyone else, but Luke didn't care that I was a bad singer. Luke didn't care about any of my weirdness, although he would never call it that.

"Where are we going?" I asked when the song finished.

"It's a secret."

"That's not fair."

"You can't be in control all the time."

"Why not?"

"Because that's not the way life works. Sometimes you have to share."

I sighed. I guess if I had to share then Luke would be the one, I'd share with. I shared everything else with him—my dreams, my fears, just about every waking hour. Why not control?

Thirty minutes later we pulled up in front of a takeaway shop.

Luke turned to me. "Fish and chips?"

"Hell yeah. I love this place."

"I know."

Of course, he did. Sometimes I thought he knew me better than I knew myself. We walked in side by side. Warmth spread through me as we stood next to each other placing our orders. When I snuck a look up at his face, my skin prickled, like my mouth would when I ate a Fruit Tingle. I took a breath in, ready to spill my guts.

What would he do if I told him? I wanted him to sweep me up in his arms and tell me I was the only one for him. That was stupid. If he felt that way, he would have told me already.

The words I love you *stuck in my throat.*

"THIS IS MORE civilised than last time," I said as Luke handed me a glass of Moscato. We sat on blankets and pillows on the tray of his ute in a secret spot beside the sandy banks of the river. We were in a small clearing surrounded by tall gum trees. Warm light from the sunset filtered through the trees bathing everything in gold. As the temperature dropped the noises of the bush increased. Birds chirped, flying from tree to tree, sharing their last thoughts for the evening. Rustling came from the leaf matter.

"I can afford more than Two Buck Chuck this time."

I glanced at the label, my heart overflowing when I read the label: Banrock Station. "You know the way to my heart."

He waved the bottle at me and grinned. "I hope I know the way to your—"

"Stomach," I said, popping the last chip in my mouth.

"Not quite."

We ate in silence, watching as the sun set over the river. Two glasses of Moscato and I was starting to feel giddy. Luke rolled up the fish and chip paper and shoved it to the side.

"Do you want another glass?" he asked.

"Are you trying to get me drunk, Luke?"

"Absolutely not. I want you to remember every last thing about tonight."

He took the glass from my hand and placed it in the Esky beside us. My heart thumped in my chest as he faced me, and his lips found mine. When his lips drew away mine felt cold and alone.

Luke wrapped his arm around my waist and pulled me down, lying beside me in one fluid motion. My lips cheered when he kissed them again. I folded my leg around his, wishing I'd worn something more accessible than jeans. The t-shirt didn't pose the same problem. Luke found my breasts through the soft material. The bra was too much of a barrier. I pushed him away, undid the clasp and slipped the straps through my sleeves, quickly discarding it.

"That's an interesting way to remove a bra."

I answered by grabbing his hand and guiding it under my t-shirt until it landed on my breast. His fingers found my nipple. He groaned before I did.

"Oh fuck," he said.

"I hope so."

His lips and hand were no longer gentle. I sighed into his mouth before I snatched at his shirt, wanting it off. He tore it off before kissing me again, his mouth rough. My nipples hardened. This was a side of Luke I'd never seen before. He was in control, taking what he wanted. His fingers found the button of my jeans. Heat spread through me. Desperate for him, I tried to shove his hand away so I could get my jeans off quicker. His hand wouldn't budge. He took mine in his and placed it by my side, his kiss never faltering. I wanted his hands on me. On my skin. When I thought I couldn't stand it anymore, he undid my button and zip with such speed he was soon pulling my jeans down. Luke grabbed them and my underwear and ripped them from my legs.

I wanted him so bad I ached for him.

CHAPTER TWENTY

Luke

Emily lay before me like a goddess waiting for the taking. Her green eyes wide and expectant. The only material left was her t-shirt. I didn't care that her whole body wasn't exposed to me. What I saw was tantalising enough. I ran my hand up her thigh to her waist and then back down through her light brown pubic hair before reaching the moistness between her legs. She raised herself to meet my fingers, her legs open. I slipped in a finger and then another. She was wet and I was rock hard in my pants.

"Luke." Her voice was soft. A moan followed as my fingers slid in and out.

"Luke." Louder this time. I took my eyes away from where my fingers were entering her and looked up at her beautiful face. She bit her bottom lip and then licked her lips. "Enough with your fingers. I want your dick inside me."

How many times had I dreamt of this? Of having sex with her in every position imaginable? And now she was begging me to take her. I thought our first time would be slow, exploring each other's bodies...hell, exploring could wait.

I undid my jeans and yanked them down. As I settled over Emily's body, she opened her legs and invited me in. I pushed my dick in inch by inch feeling her tense and then release beneath me. She moved her hips as I thrust inside her. I shifted my weight so I wasn't heavy against her. My knees and elbows pressed into the metal below the blankets.

Emily clutched my back holding me close. Her breathing was hot and fast against my ear. I thrusted faster, pressure building inside me. Slapping skin. Emily's moans. Her arching back. I drove harder and faster, the release building inside me. One last thrust. I groaned as I emptied myself inside her. Emily's nails dug into my skin as she called out my name.

I stayed there, my dick inside her as she relaxed beneath me. I stayed there until my dick softened. Then I rolled onto my back and stared up at the stars. A shooting star lit up the sky. I wished the same wish I had for as long as I could remember—I want to be best friends with Emily forever and ever.

I WALKED into the kitchen still glowing from our date the night before. Emily was nowhere to be seen.

Jim looked up from his place at the table. "Emily's hanging up the washing."

I sat down opposite him. He'd hardly touched his mash potato. That's all he could stomach these days. Sometimes he slathered it in salty butter, waiting for it to melt in. He would spoon it into his mouth and let it sit there, savouring the taste. As I watched he stirred it a bit and pushed the bowl away.

"How was your first date?"

I tried to contain my goofy smile. I didn't want to let on what we'd gotten up to.

"We had fish and chips by the river. Did some star watching."

"Sounds romantic."

I nodded.

"What's happening here, Luke? I'm going to die soon. Emily will leave. What about you?"

"I was hoping Emily would stay. Live at the farm and travel for work."

"You want Emmaline to stay in a place she hates? In a place that hates her, in a town she won't even enter?"

I didn't know how to respond. As usual, he managed to point out all of my failings without even knowing what they were. A town that hated her. A town that hated her so much they asked me to spy on her and I never told them no, even though I loved her. My stomach tightened.

"So, what you're saying is that you love her but you're not willing to sacrifice anything for that love?"

It was so much worse than that but all I uttered was, "I can't leave the farm. My parents want me to stay. I was always destined to take over."

"What about what Emily wants?" He gave me a hard stare. "What about what you want?"

Spending every day with Emily, sharing my life with her, working side by side, having a family—I could see it as clearly as if it were actually happening. Except my life was written out for me and I just accepted that I would do as expected. I'd learnt long ago not to want anything else. Except Emily. I wanted Emily. How could I have what I wanted and keep everyone happy?

"I'll find a way. I have to."

Shorty was eating off a plate next to Jim's. It almost made me laugh, how much that man loved that baby rabbit. "Shorty's grown."

"He's three times the size he was. It's probably time we take him to his new home."

It would be hard for him to say goodbye. That little bundle of fur was part of the reason his health hadn't declined rapidly. Shorty gave him purpose every day. Feeding him, keeping him warm, tending to his needs. The same things Emily did for him.

"Has Emily found somewhere for him?"

"She called a vet in NSW who said she would take him and neuter him before she adopted him out."

"That's good. We don't want to add to the rabbit population."

The screen door opened, and I turned to greet Emily. My stomach flipped as she caught my eye and smiled just for me.

I would find a way to spend every day of my life with her. I had to.

CHAPTER TWENTY-ONE

Emily

I GLANCED at Dad's bowl. He hadn't eaten anything. Maybe it was a morning thing. He had eaten last night, and a missed meal wasn't something to panic about. Except it was becoming more frequent, and it was more like one meal a day. I worried because mashed potato wasn't full of nutrients. I couldn't stop him from eating something he enjoyed though. The doctor had given him a liquid supplement and he'd suggested a nasal tube, but Dad had refused. I didn't blame him. It sounded horrible.

There wasn't much time left. We all knew that. I knew that, although I never said it out loud. It wasn't like I was in denial but speaking about it wasn't going to change it.

"Shorty is out of carrots," Dad said, turning my attention away from him and his bowl.

"I'll have to go into town to grab some."

"Into Alma?" Luke asked.

"Well, yeah. I'm not going to do a one hour plus round trip for some carrots."

They couldn't stop me from buying food, could they?

"I'll go with you."

I smiled, thankful. Luke would never make me face something so threatening on my own.

"Well, off you go. No one wants to watch you two make lovey dovey eyes at each other all day." Dad stood up. "I'm going to sit outside while you're gone."

He made his way out, using the chairs and wall for stability. I gathered up Shorty and put him in his box with his food then topped up his water and took him outside.

"Put him in the play pen. Let him be a rabbit for a while," Dad said.

Dad sat down in the lounge chair we'd brought out onto the porch for him. It was more comfortable for him seeing he was mostly skin and bone. If he fell asleep it would cushion him. Luke put a plastic cup of water on the table beside him. We'd all stopped using glass after Dad had a couple of accidents.

"We'll be back soon," I said, bending down and giving him a kiss on the cheek.

"Don't hurry back on my account. I'm not going anywhere." He gave me a weak smile.

"When are you taking Shorty to NSW?" Luke asked as he sat in the passenger seat.

"Soon. He's big enough now."

I was hesitant though. Every day I swayed between keeping him for Dad or taking him to his new home. I didn't think getting caught with him would be a problem. No one visited except Luke and his family, and Aisha and Dalir. But I was sure buying more rabbit food would raise some questions.

"You could keep him for a bit longer. Your dad will miss him."

"I know. I'm worried Dad will get worse without him." I blew my breath out puffing up my cheeks. Luke reached over and gave my leg a rub. Luke understood. He always did.

I parked out the front of the supermarket and unclenched my fingers from around the steering wheel. This whole town had the same effect on me. I swear it could give a person an ulcer.

Luke opened his door. "Come on."

I didn't hesitate. Having Luke with me was enough to reassure me that nothing could touch me here. He was like a forcefield. We could have each other and everyone else could get stuffed. As soon as I stepped onto the footpath, he held my hand. The sliding doors slid open, and we walked inside. Everyone at the registers turned around and stared at us. It was like some sort of stupid joke; a man and a woman walk into a supermarket...I clenched my teeth and strode to the fruit and veg.

"Do we just need carrots?" Luke asked as he grabbed a bag.

I shook my head. "As much as Dad thinks that's all Shorty wants to eat, it's not healthy for him. We need some broccoli, spinach and celery."

Luke let go of my hand to get what we needed. I grabbed a bag of potatoes for Dad. When I turned back to Luke some farmer had approached him and was patting him on the shoulder. I watched his lips as he spoke and was sure he said 'good job'.

"What was that about?" I asked Luke as he returned to my side.

He shrugged, not making eye contact with me. "Have we got everything to make Shorty a happy boy?"

I laughed. That little rabbit had us all under his command.

"I'm sure Shorty will be satisfied."

We made our way to the check out. I didn't recognise the lady serving but she sure seemed to know me. Her critical gaze as she looked me up and down told me that. She looked between Luke and I, a weird smile on her face. What was with these people? Had they never seen a happy couple before?

"Oh, look, the two L's." Bianca's saccharine voice made me cringe. I didn't even know she was in the shop. I don't know how I could miss her when there were only four aisles. My Bianca radar had failed me.

Luke placed his hand on the small of my back as we walked forward. "Just ignore her. She wants you to respond."

I nodded. Ignoring her was something I did well. Had done for my whole school life.

I paid, and the girl at the register half-smiled. "Bye Lemony. Hope you have a lovely day with your *boyfriend*."

Bianca laughed her ugly laugh and said loud enough for everyone to hear, "Did you see what she bought? All those vegetables aren't going to help her fat arse."

Instinct took over. I turned to her. What was her problem? Why couldn't she just let go of her stupid childhood grudge?

"Oh, you heard that. Awks."

I tensed. Luke kept guiding me forward. He let me go out the front door before he turned back to them. "You're a bitch."

I watched for Bianca's response through the window. She winked at Luke and blew him a kiss before giving me a smarmy smile and turning away.

The celery crunched under my fingers as I clenched it. I don't know if I was angrier at myself for not speaking up, letting her get to me or if it was that fucking wink she'd given Luke. I took a deep breath and turned to the car. I didn't want her to see how much she had gotten to me, even though my face would have already given me away.

Luke let me stew. He knew me well, too well. I'd never win a fight with him, but I was about to pick one anyway.

"Why didn't you let me stick up for myself?"

"It wouldn't have ended well."

"So? It never ends well. She always fucking wins."

Luke sighed.

Heat screamed through my veins. "And what was that fucking wink all about?"

"You know what she's like. She knows how to push your buttons."

"I didn't see you objecting."

"What?"

Twenty years of pent-up anger came to the surface. "You've never objected to her advances."

"Don't be ridiculous."

"Ridiculous? Fuck off, Luke." I was swearing like a sailor and couldn't care less.

"What do you want me to do? Tell her to piss off?"

"Well, it wouldn't hurt."

"Are you sure about that?"

I turned my glare on him.

"Think about it. Your reaction has always been bait to her.

Imagine what would happen if I reacted. She'd push harder."
Luke watched me.

"Would she? It might actually show them that you think I'm worthy enough to fight for." What was I even saying? Luke always stuck up for me. Nothing I was thinking made sense.

My fingers ached but I couldn't let go of the steering wheel, not even to flex them. It was like they were fused there. My whole body was fused. Every joint stiff. Every muscle tensed.

I pulled off to the side of the road and got out of the car in a rush of limbs and angst. Luke followed. I wanted to punch him. He kept his distance, waiting, as if he knew I needed to figure this out on my own.

"I'm angry at you. I'm angry at myself. All my life, I've let you protect me. I need to stand up for myself."

Luke stood, passive. I wanted to pound my fists into his chest, for him to show me something. I needed to see this affect him for a change. I don't know what I wanted exactly, maybe some anger or frustration. Some sort of emotion other than his continuing calmness.

"You're right. I should have let you say something."

His admission didn't help the heat in my veins.

"These people, this town has always made me feel unworthy, pathetic. I gave them that power. I gave her that power."

BIANCA CORNERED me in the bathroom at school. She stood in the doorway while I washed my hands. I pretended I hadn't seen her but we both knew I had. My furtive glances *were a dead giveaway. I made my way to the door and tried to step around her, but she blocked my path.*

"You think you're pretty good, don't you?"

I didn't engage. I'd learnt long ago, the more I replied, the nastier she got.

"You think that scholarship means anything?"

It did mean something. It meant someone believed in me. For once I was brave enough to raise my eyes to hers.

"It means jack shit. Except that Luke can get rid of you without having to get rid of you."

I flinched. An evil smile lifted her lips.

"You can't think that Luke is interested in you, in poor little Emmaline."

I'd never thought Luke was interested in me. He was my best friend. A best friend I loved, but I'd never say those words out loud.

"Oh my God, Emmaline. You're pathetic."

She reached out. Her evil smile spreading as I shrunk away from her hand. It didn't stop her from tapping my face.

"Pathetic."

LUKE STOOD WATCHING me as tears streamed down my face.

"I loved you, Luke. With all of me, I loved you. She knew. They all knew. And all she did was tell me I was pathetic."

Luke clenched his jaw. A vein popped out on his neck. He made to move towards me, but my next words stopped him.

"I'm worthy, Luke. I'm worthy of love. I'm worthy of a

good happy life. I won't let them take that away from me anymore."

When I finished, Luke closed the distance between us and wrapped me in his arms. "You're more than worthy."

I cried in his arms. Cried all the tears I'd kept inside for too many years. As my tears slowed, my resolve strengthened. No more.

Luke kissed the top of my head. "I love you. I've always loved you."

Those words didn't make sense. He pulled away and looked down at me.

"Maybe I should have told you. I don't know. I didn't want to hold you back." He sighed. "You needed to be free of this place. You had a better life to live."

Dad. Luke. They were both the same. Withholding their words, their feelings, so I would leave them. I'd never really left. My heart had been with them while my passion, my life and my body were elsewhere. Luke put a finger under my chin and lifted my face. His lips met mine. Gentle. Full of promise.

CHAPTER TWENTY-TWO

Luke

I SAT at the kitchen table with my parents. I wanted to speak but the words wouldn't come. Mum sat, drinking her tea. Dad read the paper. I stared down at the wooden surface. Dad laid the paper on the table and rested his hands on top. "Are you going to tell us what's wrong or are we just going to sit here in silence?"

"Emily and I went into town today."

Mum's cup banged down onto the table and she clasped her hands in front of it. "And?"

I told them what had happened.

"It made me sick. The guilt I had when a farmer came up and told me I was doing a good job. The way Bianca insulted her and threw me a kiss afterwards."

Dad stiffened.

"I called her a bitch, but she didn't take it seriously. She thought it was all part of her sick game."

Mum sat back in her chair and crossed her arms.

"Emily broke down on the way home."

"It's a wonder that poor girl didn't break down years ago."

"I always thought I was protecting her. Even now."

Mum shook her head. "Do you still think that?"

"No. It's bullshit. All those lies I told to myself. I was just too afraid of—of—I don't know."

"So, what are you going to do?" Dad asked.

"I need to tell them enough is enough."

"Good." He rubbed his hands together. "Looks like we have a meeting to go to."

I did a double take. Dad hadn't been to a meeting all year. My heart rate increased at the implications. I don't know if I was nervous because I was finally going to stand up to the town or because he'd be there witnessing it. I wasn't going to allow them to trap me again. More importantly, I wouldn't let them put Emily down like they had for years.

Dad ushered us to the car and then, with equally as much enthusiasm, led us to the hall.

I squared my shoulders as I walked in for the confrontation that was sure to ensue. I spotted Bianca straight away. She was waiting for us, facing the doorway, dressed in skin-tight jeans and a white t-shirt that was so tight it left nothing to the imagination. The moment we stepped in the door she made her way toward us. Her hips swayed; more like her whole body swayed. I took a breath in, steeling myself. She kept me in her sights and gave Mum and Dad a glance when she arrived at my side. She leant in to kiss me. I stepped back so quick I nearly fell over. She paid no attention.

"Luke, your acting was superb today. You play the part of double-agent well."

"I—"

"That parting comment calling me a bitch was sublime. I bet Emily felt comforted by those words."

"I—"

"She really does need to eat more vegetables." She wrinkled her nose.

I couldn't get a word in as she continued. "I was confused about this Shorty you kept referring to. Who's Shorty?"

"A rab—"

"Bianca, I think your mother wants you," Mum said, looking towards the front of the room. Fucking Bianca. I'd nearly let it slip about Shorty, all because I wanted to at least get one word in. That one syllable I let out would be enough for her to be able to put it together.

Mum pulled me to our chairs.

"She's a piece of work, that one," Dad grumbled.

Bianca and Mrs Phillips kept looking our way. Bianca was talking and Mrs Phillips had that know-it-all smile, nodding slowly. What had I done?

I pulled my phone out of my pocket. "I need to text Emily. I need to tell her I stuffed up."

Mum rested her hand on my arm. "Do it afterwards. Pretend you have no idea what they're up to."

She was right. I needed to play dumb. Let them believe they had all the time in the world to dob Emily and Jim in about Shorty.

"I don't know what to do now," I said softly. "I want to tell them all where to go. What if that makes them more blood thirsty?"

Dad looked at me, his face hardening. I held the stare of his steel blue eyes.

"No, I'm not changing my plans. I don't want to deceive

Emily anymore. She needs to know what's been happening and I can't tell her until I've stopped playing their game."

I was rambling and I knew it. Mum patted my arm.

"OK everyone. Time for the meeting to start. Please take your seats."

I sat up tall and planted my feet firmly on the ground. My whole body was set.

"Luke, Bianca tells me you've got some news to share with us."

Unbelievable. There was no pretence that this was a normal meeting where we would discuss farming related matters. Nope. Their main topic was Emily.

I stood up. All faces turned towards me. I took in a deep breath. "I'm not spying on Emily. I'm not pretending to date her. I never agreed to your stupid plan."

Heads swung from me to Mrs Phillips.

"We understand, Luke. It has been a lot to ask of you."

"Yeah, pretending to like Emily would be torture," Bianca said.

Dad shifted in his seat. Mum put a hand on his leg to settle him.

"I like Emily just fine. She is a good person. I enjoy spending time with her."

"What?" Bianca stood up.

I addressed her. "I don't need to pretend to like Emily or to date Emily. I love Emily and I am dating her."

"Don't be ridiculous."

"You are the one who's being ridiculous. Emily has come home to look after Jim. That's it. She doesn't care about you or your farms."

"Bullshit."

"No, Bianca, it's the truth."

"Then why was she at St Clair giving a talk?"

In my peripheral vision I could see people nodding. Brainwashed idiots.

"She was invited."

She screwed her nose up. "As if."

I had so much more to say but I remembered Emily's words. It wasn't my place to say them. That was her fight. My fight was telling them I wasn't going to play their games anymore.

I turned to my parents. "Let's go."

EMILY AND JIM were sitting on the porch when we pulled up to their house. Emily's smile when she greeted us had me shaking. I was about to tell her I'd betrayed her trust—I knew I hadn't *actually* spied on her but that was beside the point. They all thought I was going to. I looked between her and Jim. I couldn't tell her in front of him. One of them being angry with me would be bad enough.

"Let's go for a walk," I said to her when I reached the top step. I couldn't even look at Jim. Mum made her way to Emily's chair and Dad stood against the railing.

We walked the track to the river. I'd thought about how I'd start the conversation on the drive over. Those words escaped me. We kept walking until we reached the river.

"I'm sorry, Emily."

Her eyebrows drew together.

Good way to start, dickhead.

I pointed to a rock. "Sit."

I paced in front of her before I realised I couldn't stand while she sat. Standing was a sign of dominance. It would shift the balance of power. I sat on a rock opposite her.

"What are you sorry for, Luke?"

"When Mum and I went to our first farmers co-op meeting after you came home, they asked me to spy on you."

I tried to gauge her reaction. Nothing.

"I figured if they thought I'd said yes, they'd leave you alone. I didn't need to spy on you, I'd be with you anyway. I just thought I'd be able to control the narrative."

Excuses. They were just excuses.

Still, she said nothing.

"So, then we went back, and you know how Bianca twists things. She told them all I was fake dating you to get more information."

Emily sucked her breath in. "Fake dating me?"

"Well, yeah." I rubbed the back of my neck.

Her green eyes narrowed. "And you never thought to correct them?"

"I did. Tonight."

"But not back then. You let them believe you didn't even care for me."

I tried to swallow the lump of guilt in my throat. It wouldn't budge. She'd spent so much of her life thinking she wasn't worthy, that she was pathetic. And my actions, my stupidity, could bring all that back. My words, my declaration of love, were just empty words.

"There's more."

"More? How much more could you betray me?"

Could it get worse? Yes, as soon as I opened my mouth.

"I sort of let slip about Shorty."

"You did what?"

"I didn't mean to. Bianca was at me..."

It didn't matter what I said. There was nothing to justify it.

Emily stood up. She started to walk back to the house.

"Emily, wait."

She turned back to me. Her scowling face red.

"Don't speak to me, Luke."

"Please, Emily. I didn't mean to."

She strode back to me. Her voice shook. Her whole body shook. "What didn't you mean to do, Luke? You didn't mean to appease those people by betraying me? You forgot to stick up for me when you had the chance? Tell them your feelings for me?"

She stared at me waiting.

When I didn't speak, she said, "You didn't mean to do all that? Or you didn't mean to lie to me and have sex with me? Or you didn't mean to tell me you loved me?"

The skin on her face tightened as her mouth curled into a snarl. A microsecond later her face fell, and she threw up her hands.

"Or you didn't mean to take the one thing my father is living for away?"

I swallowed. The nausea was rising. The realisation of everything I was about to lose slammed into me.

I reached out for her. "Emily—"

She stepped out of my grasp.

"Don't touch me, Luke. Don't speak to me. You've said enough."

Or more like I hadn't said enough.

CHAPTER TWENTY-THREE

Emily

I STORMED UP THE STAIRS, not daring to look at anyone. Tears threatened to fall, and I was afraid that, with one kind word, the dam would break. That was not going to happen. I'd cried in front of Luke and where had that gotten me? Pain and lies.

I was so stupid to think Luke was interested in me, let alone loved me. Bianca was right. I was pathetic. They were all probably laughing at me now.

Everything that had happened in the supermarket fell into place.

I closed the door to my room and let the tears flow. I threw myself onto my bed. Big fat tears escaped, and I gulped for air while snot poured onto my pillow. It was safe in here, safe to let my feelings free. Out there I would never let them know how they'd broken me. Luke especially. Luke and Bianca were in this together. I was so stupid.

There was only one other time I'd felt this betrayed.

. . .

LUKE and I were sitting on the hot school bus. The windows were open allowing air to flow but it made little difference on the hot summer day. Sweat pooled in the small of my back and under my legs. I couldn't decide what was worse the sliminess of the sweat against the vinyl or how my uniform was getting wet.

Our stop was the furthest away so as we got closer to school the bus filled up. My dress was faded compared to the other girls', as Bianca had pointed out many a time. Almost everything I owned was a hand me down.

Everyone who boarded the bus greeted Luke but didn't even acknowledge my presence. My heart sank. This year was going to be the same as every other year. Bianca and her popularity won out again. She could turn people against a nun. I should have been used to it. I was as insignificant at school among my peers as I was at home. It didn't matter as long as I had Luke. Being with him for two hours every day on the school bus made the trip bearable.

Bianca hopped on the bus and sat in front of us with her friend. Their chatter caught my attention. They went from loud to quiet, to giggles and furtive glances at Luke. Normally Luke would look at me and we would have a wordless conversation about how annoying their presence was. When I glanced at him, he was smiling at them. Then he leant forward, braced his arms on the top of his seat and started talking to them, looking at some football cards they were showing him.

Bianca looked at me and gave me a 'suck it, bitch' smile.

. . .

LUKE'S CAR STARTED. I took deep breaths, calming myself. I needed to go out to help Dad. He couldn't get to bed by himself and he would need help getting changed. I went to the bathroom and washed my face, getting rid of the mucous and trying to eliminate the red splotches. Thank goodness my hair was short. I'd hate to imagine trying to clean that mess out of it. Taking a deep breath, I closed my eyes. I could do this. I could do all of this, by myself. Dad, the farm, everything.

Dad looked up at me as I came out the back door. He gave me a small smile. At least something was good in the world. Us.

"Do you want to talk about it?"

"Not yet." I wasn't sure I'd ever be ready.

He nodded. The understanding on his face told me that Luke's parents had filled him in.

"Are you ready for bed?"

"Yes."

I removed the blanket from his lap. Dad shuffled to the front of the chair. We had graduated from the lounge chair to a higher one with arms. It was easier for him to move in it and easier for me to help him up. I waited for him to move his feet back, so they were nearly beneath him. He paused while I moved to the side and positioned myself so my feet were wide and legs were bent. I placed my arm under his and lifted while I guided him forward with my other hand.

"Do you need the wheelchair?" I should have asked before he'd stood up, but I hadn't been thinking straight.

"Not today. My legs are feeling restless."

We shuffled to his room. I imagined how frustrating it was for him, being so nimble once and now moving so slowly. He never complained. Never demanded anything. I helped him into a sitting position on his bed and waited for him to take his shirt off. He only wore button shirts now, as they were easier than him taking a t-shirt off over his head. I helped him into his sleep shirt and his pyjama shorts.

"Thank you, Emily."

"You're welcome."

"Luke said he will be here in the morning to help me shower."

"OK. I'll make sure I've left the house by then."

Dad patted my hand before lying down.

I collected Shorty from his enclosure outside and put him in his cage. I wasn't letting him wreak havoc that night. He had a thing for chewing electrical cords—my laptop charger, the lamp, the fridge. It was a wonder he didn't electrocute himself.

I WOKE up the same way I'd gone to sleep, tossing and turning, and clenching my teeth. I was grateful Luke was coming to help Dad but that's where my positive thoughts stopped. I didn't want to see him or speak to him. That kiss Bianca had blown to him kept playing over and over in my mind. Along with the words fake dating.

Luke had been in on it the whole time and the realisation that he'd been happy to get rid of me when I'd gone to uni, just like Bianca said, crashed into me with such force my insides collapsed.

I went into Dad's room and gave him a gentle shake. He smiled when he opened his eyes and saw me standing beside him.

"Do you want breakfast now?"

"Not yet."

I didn't like him not eating but it didn't mean he wouldn't. He just took longer to get up and going these days.

"I'm going out to cut the millet. Do you want to get up or wait for Luke here?"

"I'll come out and wait. I'm sure Shorty would like some sunshine."

"You know, now that Luke has told them about Shorty, we'll have to take him soon."

"I know."

I set Dad and Shorty up, made some toast and headed out to the shed. I ate as I hooked up the harvester to the tractor. I tried not to think about the last time I was in the tractor with Luke and how much his touch excited me. His touch that must have been a lie. I pushed the tears away.

Row after row of millet was cut. It was a form of meditation: up, down, up, down. I emptied my mind and watched the ground disappear below me.

Hours later, I finished. My stomach dropped when I returned to the shed and saw Luke's car still in the driveway. I couldn't have been any clearer when I'd said I didn't want to talk to him. Maybe he had another lie ready to shove in my face.

I took my phone out of my pocket. There were three messages from an unknown number. I opened them. I broke into a sweat as I stared at photos of Luke and Bianca. They were undeniably Luke, with his trademark messy blond hair. Bianca with her arm around Luke's, looking up into his face. Luke looking down Bianca's top. Luke and Bianca kissing.

CHAPTER TWENTY-FOUR

Luke

EMILY THUNDERED up the steps and ripped the screen door open. I shrunk back in my chair as she turned to me, pure hatred on her face.

"You can tell your fucking girlfriend not to send me any more photos." She threw her phone down on the table. A photo stared up at me. A photo of Bianca and I kissing. Only that had never happened.

"I'm sure you two are having a good laugh. You can get fucked."

I scrolled through the other photos. That bitch set me up.

"Emily, these—"

"I'm going to have a shower. When I get out, I want you gone. I don't want to see you, Luke. Ever."

She left the room and Jim reached out his hand. I gave him the phone.

"They're not real," I blurted out.

"I hope not." Jim studied me. "Because if they were, our friendship would be over."

I got up and paced. How was I going to convince Emily that these photos weren't real? They sure looked real. There was no way to tell her when she wouldn't even speak to me.

Heat spread through me, and I shook. Bianca had ruined my life and I had held her hand the whole damn way. I was as much to blame here as she was. I always wanted to keep the peace. I never wanted confrontation. I never wanted to disappoint anyone. And now I'd disappointed the most important person in my life. Not just disappointed her. I'd hurt her.

I was an idiot.

"I'm so fucking angry with myself. I wasted all those years and then, when I had a glimpse of happiness, I threw it all away."

"That's the smartest thing I've heard you say."

"This is my fault for letting them manipulate me."

"Yes."

I appreciated his bluntness.

I sank down onto my chair and rested my head in my hands. I couldn't fix this with Emily today. Maybe never. She was too angry, and she had every right to be.

I held out my hand to Jim and he gave me the phone. I texted the pictures to myself in case I needed proof.

I stood up; the table wobbled as I knocked it. I strode to the door.

"Where are you going?"

"I'm going to sort Bianca out for once and for all."

Those photos rolled around in my mind. Bianca must have been planning this from the beginning. I bet her arsehole brother had a hand in it. I needed to think this through. I needed to do this in a way that Bianca would forever leave me, no us, alone. Firstly, I needed to calm down. If she saw she'd gotten a rise out of me, it would feed her ego. Next, it needed to be done in public. I wasn't sure how I was going to swing that one. Then I needed to be as clear as glass in my message.

Keep calm. Do it in public. Be clear.

Bianca's car wasn't at the rural supplies. I drove into the main street looking for the little pink car. It was outside the supermarket. I parked out the front. Breathing in deep, I reminded myself: stay calm and be clear.

Bianca was gossiping at the register with the checkout chick and a guy. The owner was hovering around filling the shelves near the register and there were a couple of people shopping. This would need to be public enough.

Bianca leant against the counter with her hip, hair tossed over her shoulder and chest protruding. I rolled my eyes. She had no shame.

She didn't change position as I approached. Not until I stood amongst them. Then she stood straight and turned to face me directly. I swallowed down the lump in my throat and made a conscious effort not to step back.

"Hello Luke," she said sweetly.

Stay calm. Be clear.

"Bianca."

"Did Emily get the photos I sent her?"

"She was amused by your desperation." My voice was even, nonchalant.

Bianca watched me. Her lack of words showed me I was on the right track. Calm. Stay calm.

"I suggest you don't contact her anymore."

Her hands went to her hips. "I'll do what I like."

I shrugged. "Don't say I didn't warn you. She'll have no qualms about reporting you for using a carriage service to harass her."

Bianca stared at me blankly. She couldn't be that dumb if she managed to set me up the way she did.

"Electronic communication." I couldn't hold back the sarcasm in my voice. "And those photos you doctored; I suggest you destroy them. Because if they turn up anywhere else, we have evidence they came from you."

Her jaw set and she tossed her hair. This was good. A thinking Bianca, with no come back, was just what I wanted.

"I want to be very clear with you so you can't misconstrue what I'm saying." I was aware of everyone watching us. My voice was loud enough for them all to hear. "I am not interested in you. I have never been interested in you. I want you to stay out of my and Emily's lives."

I walked away.

"You can have each other. You're both losers."

I kept walking, resisting the urge to give her the finger.

I WALKED into the refuge looking for Robbie. I found him in the office, his red head bent over some paperwork. When I entered, he looked up at me and frowned. "You look like shit."

"I fucked up." I sank down into the chair opposite him.

He got up and went to the fridge, coming back with two beers. I took one and cracked it open. Taking a swig, I savoured the bitterness as the amber liquid slid down my throat.

"Are you going to elaborate?"

When I finished telling him the sordid details, he whistled. "Yeah, fucked up doesn't quite cover it."

I drowned the beer in two gulps, and he got me another. There wasn't enough beer in the world to get rid of the dread in my stomach.

"I don't know what to do. I thought everything was falling into place. That my dreams had come true."

"The love dome was impressive."

My head snapped up. "The what?"

"The love dome. You two were so into each other that nothing else mattered."

"Yeah. It was like a drug."

"But what was going to happen when you stepped out of the dome?"

What was he getting at? "We're out of it now."

My stomach sank further because no matter how I thought about it I knew that this was going to be hard to come back from. The first battle would be proving the photos weren't real. The next would be getting Emily to actually speak to me. Even if I did that, how could she forgive me?

"But if this hadn't happened, what did the future hold for you?"

"Love. Marriage. Kids."

"And where would you have these kids?"

He was right. Robbie was always right. "I don't know. I didn't think that far ahead."

"I'm not saying there is hope, because if I was Emily, I'd kick you in the balls. More than once. Let's just say she loves you enough to give you another chance, what are you going to do with that chance?"

Not fuck it up. "Show her that she's more important than anything."

He nodded and waited for more. I knew exactly what he was getting at. It was the same thing Jim kept prompting me about. It didn't matter where we lived as long as we were *together*. Stay. All I needed to do was stay with her.

"Talk about the future. Where we're going to live. What we're going to do."

"How many babies you're going to have?" He grinned.

"The answer is lots."

He sighed, loud. "Remember the discuss word...don't you think you need to discuss it?"

CHAPTER TWENTY-FIVE

Emily

"Don't you stick up for him," I said to Dad. I gave him the sternest look I could muster before turning my attention back to the road.

"I wasn't."

"Really? Telling me the photos aren't real isn't sticking up for him?"

"No. It's stating a fact."

"A fact?"

"Yes. Luke told me they weren't real."

"And Luke is such an honest person that you believe him? He pretended to date me to appease some backward arse country fucks."

"That doesn't make the photos real."

"They looked pretty real to me."

"Bernie said they weren't."

That was true. She'd come over the next day and explained each of them to me. The one of them kissing, the worst one, was Bianca leaning in at the co-op meeting. It was just the right angle to look like they were kissing. Bernie wouldn't lie to me. Not even to protect Luke.

"And then he told them about Shorty."

Dad stared out the windscreen, working his jaw. "I don't think he meant to tell them about Shorty."

Maybe not. I wasn't going to admit it.

"Yet, here we are, driving to NSW to take Shorty to a new home because he *did* tell them." I reached over and patted Shorty, who was on Dad's lap.

"It had to happen sooner or later." Dad yawned.

I gripped the steering wheel. How could he forgive Luke for this? For all of it. I didn't care if he thought Luke was doing the right thing. Maybe at first it was the right thing...no, it wasn't. He should have stood up to them. He should have told them where to stick it. He'd always stuck up for me before. Or did he only do that in my presence? Had he been playing me all along?

I turned to Dad. His head was tilted back, mouth open, sleeping. He didn't stay awake for long periods anymore.

I don't know what I was supposed to think. The same thing kept running through my mind. Luke had betrayed me. He'd proved once and for all that I was pathetic. I had no right believing I was worthy of anything. I *was* worthy. Luke loving me or not loving me didn't change that. I was a good person. I deserved good things.

My thoughts went around in circles. I just kept thinking about the same thing, over and over.

"Are you still stewing over there?" Dad asked an hour later, breaking into my broken record of thoughts.

"Yes."

"Want to talk about it?"

"Maybe."

The words wouldn't come. I was too scared to say them out loud. Too scared to admit my feelings to my own father.

"I'm sorry, Emmaline."

My eyes narrowed. "What for?"

"For everything. For changing your name. For not giving you all the love you deserved. For pushing you away. For creating this insecurity you have."

He should have been sorry years ago, not just now. "Why? Because you're dying?" The words came out, and although they shouldn't have, I didn't want to take them back.

"No, because I was an arse."

Well, that was the truth.

"When you were lying there in that hospital bed, I had a lot of time to think and wallow in self-pity. Seeing you, lying there broken, was too much."

Dad had never spoken to me about that time. I'd been in a coma for months, enough time for my broken bones to heal.

"One day I just decided to change your name. Your mum loved that name. Every time I said it, it reminded me of her."

I closed my eyes. Mum's voice sounded in my head. Her beautiful voice saying my name as if it were part of a song or poetry.

"But it was selfish. I took away part of your identity."

When I'd woken up, I'd been in a strange place. No Mum to reassure me everything would be OK. Just a distant, scared father who called me a new name. When my brothers and sister came to visit, they would get into trouble if they called me Emmaline. They tried to make things normal for me at home, but I guess it was hard for them. Their mum had died, and their father was a changed man. He spent more time out of the house than with us.

"Although I loved you with every fibre of my being, I didn't want you to know. You were different to the others. They couldn't wait to leave, to start their own life away from the farm and it wasn't long before they did. But you, you would have stayed."

I nodded. I could very easily have been a homebody. The farm connected me to Mum. And I had Luke.

"But I couldn't let you stay. Not in that dreaded place. A place where people were full of negativity. Your mum and I had planned to leave, we wanted a better future for you all, but farm prices had dropped drastically with the drought and we were quietly waiting for them to rise."

I glanced at him.

"We didn't tell anyone except Luke's parents. If people knew, they'd make life difficult."

Make life difficult? It shouldn't surprise me. Those hateful people controlled our lives in more than one way.

"After your mum died, I never found the right time to leave. I didn't care about the money. I didn't stay because of that. You and Luke were inseparable. He was like a shining beacon for you. All I could give you, if we left, was me. And you were doing so well in school. The teachers would rave at parent teacher interviews. I didn't want to jeopardise your future."

"So, we stayed."

"Until you left."

Tears welled in my eyes. All of this time I'd thought he didn't love me. Yet, he'd sacrificed a lot for me. Dad reached over and squeezed my leg. I took his hand. It was so much to take in. Him and Luke. His unspoken love. Luke's spoken love. One was true. The other wasn't.

"I know what Luke did hurt you. If I had the strength, I'd slap him upside of the head."

"I believed him, Dad. I believed him when he told me he loved me."

"He does love you."

"How can you say that after what he's done?"

"We all make mistakes."

I blew out my breath and stared at the black road with the cloudless sky looking down on us. Not all mistakes were that bad.

"When your mum and I first started seeing each other, there was another guy interested in her. I wasn't prepared to compete. I felt it was below me, that she should have just chosen me. So, I told him he could have her."

"You did what?" I let go of his hand and he returned it to Shorty.

"Oh yeah, your mum was furious." He chuckled. I didn't see how it was funny. "She didn't let the other guy think he'd won her by default. She made him work for it."

Go Mum.

"I pretended I didn't care, but it ate me up inside. I watched and I sulked. She didn't pay me any attention. Why would she? My actions had shown her I didn't care."

My heart beat fast. How horrible. By not even thinking about fighting for her, he had rejected her to her face. I smiled, then laughed. He may have rejected her, but she had the upper hand. She was happy and he was miserable.

"I watched them get closer and I got angrier every day. I

realised what a damn fool I'd been, thinking someone like your mum didn't deserve the world."

She deserved the world, the moon and the stars.

"I took her for granted. I took the fact that her mere presence brightened my day for granted. I took the way her smile lifted me for granted. After I gave myself a stern talk, I never took her for granted again."

It was true. I remembered our house full of love. The way Dad would look at her as if she was the reason the sun rose every day. How he would tell her that she made the best mashed potato in the world. He'd thank her for helping on the farm or for being such a good mum. He'd give her a kiss as they did the dishes together. How they'd share smiles as one or the other helped with homework while the other cooked dinner.

Everything Dad did, Mum did in return.

"Do you think that you may take Luke for granted?"

Did I take Luke for granted? I always expected him to stick up for me. Always expected him to be there. Always expected him to take my call or listen to me. Expected. I expected him to. And the one time he didn't do what I expected…

"Maybe."

Dad rested his head against the window. I reached into the back seat and grabbed his pillow for him.

"Partners are going to make mistakes. Your mum and I made plenty."

"I suppose."

"Do you love Luke? Or is he just your best friend who's always been there for you?"

"Both."

"I can tell you without a doubt that Luke loves you. He's always loved you."

I gave him a sidelong glance. How did Dad know this when I had no clue?

He shook his head. "You are so dense. Everyone in the world could see it except the two of you."

What was he even talking about?

"When you achieved something, who was the first person there to congratulate you? When he saw you every morning, who had the biggest smile on his face? Who sat with you on the bus every single day? Who has been helping you on the farm? Who can't wait to see you every day? Who was the first person you told when you learnt something new? Who made you happier than a pig in shit?"

I smiled.

"Luke." It was all Luke. Even now, it was Luke.

Dad yawned.

"Do you want to go on living without him?"

"No."

"Good."

After thirty seconds of silence, I looked over at Dad. He was asleep again, cradling Shorty in his lap, who was also asleep.

CHAPTER TWENTY-SIX

Luke

I WAITED on the verandah for Emily and Jim to arrive home. The sun had begun its descent and the golden light spread across the fields. This time of night was glorious. I didn't want to enjoy it alone anymore.

Emily's ute turned into the driveway. I stood up and went to the railing. Sweat broke out across my skin. Thank goodness for deodorant. Emily ignored me as she helped Jim into his wheelchair. She ignored me as she pushed him up the ramp, we'd made a couple of weeks ago.

Jim didn't ignore me. "Luke."

"Hi, Jim, did the trip go well?"

"Yes, Shorty will be well taken care of."

"That's good."

He looked up at Emily. "Can you make me some dinner please? I'll eat inside."

She nodded.

As she pushed him toward the door, I opened it for them.

"Thank you." She glanced at me as she made her way inside.

I breathed a sigh of relief at the first words she'd spoken to me in days.

Before being pushed inside, Jim said, "Don't stuff this up."

I wouldn't. I couldn't.

Leaning against the railing, I watched the shadows through the screen door. Beeps from the microwave indicated the mash was ready. More movement. More shadows. She was coming out, wasn't she?

Finally, the screen door opened. Emily made eye contact with me as she came out. She stopped in front of me, close enough to touch. I didn't dare reach out to her. Not yet.

"I know I did the wrong thing. I should have said no right at the beginning, and I should have told you."

"Yes, you should have."

She was talking. This was good.

"Those photos weren't real."

"Your mother said so."

I nodded. What else was there to do?

"Do you always send your mum in to fight your battles?" Her hands went to her hips.

"Only the important ones."

I wasn't ashamed of it. Emily wouldn't listen to me, but she would listen to my mum. Hell, I'd send my dad in to battle if all else failed.

She folded her arms and pursed her lips. "And my dad, was he part of your strategy, too?"

"Sometimes you need to pull out the big guns." He'd told me he would speak to her when she was ready. Perhaps today was that day. I gave her half a smile before I said, "I'm not interested in Bianca. I've told her to leave us alone."

"Right."

She wasn't giving me anything.

A bang came from inside. "Will you hurry up? A man could die waiting for you."

Emily smirked and raised her eyebrows at me.

"I love you. I loved you before I even knew what love was." I ran my hand through my hair. "I'll love you even when I'm dead. It will be inside me, always."

"That's a big statement." Her tone was flat. Her lips twitched. Was she taking the piss?

I took hold of her arm and yanked her toward me. She didn't object. Not to my arms around her. Or my lips devouring hers.

"I WONDER WHO THAT IS," I said, pointing to the car that pulled up out the front of Emily's house.

"Government car," Jim said.

We watched as a middle-aged, balding man got out of the car and came towards us. Emily stood up and met him at the bottom of the stairs.

"Hello, can I help you?"

"I'm Elliot from the Department of Agriculture and Fisheries. Are you Emily Watson?"

"Yes."

About time they'd turned up. We'd been waiting, knowing they were coming but never knowing when. It'd been a month since the farming co-op meeting. I bet Mrs Phillips had called them again seeing as they had a meeting tonight. Jim sat up straight in his seat. That's all he could manage. I rearranged the pillow behind him.

"We've had a report that you're keeping a pet rabbit on the premises."

"No pet rabbit here."

"We have people saying you've been buying vegetables for the rabbit at the supermarket?"

I rolled my eyes.

"Vegetables, you say? Well, some people in town had been commenting about my weight, so I thought I should buy some rabbit food to help. Do you think it worked?" Emily opened her arms wide inviting the investigator to look.

He blushed. "Right...um...it—" He looked down at his pad. "It also says here that Luke Baird told the witnesses you have a rabbit. Would you care to explain that?"

Emily turned to me. "Luke, is there a rabbit here?"

"Luke." Jim's voice was raspy. Where had that come from? He'd never been raspy before.

We all turned our attention to Jim.

"Ask the man to—" Jim took a breath in "—come here."

The investigator looked down at his feet. He tapped the pad against his hand. Emily shifted to the side and swept her hand towards the stairs. He did as requested.

"We don't have—" Breath "—a rabbit here."

Jim broke into a racking cough, gulping in air. "No rabbit here."

Jim stared at the man. Even I felt uncomfortable, and I knew he was faking it all.

"Thank you, sir. There's obviously been a mistake." He looked at the three of us. "I'm sorry to have disturbed you."

He started backing away.

"Tell those busy bodies—" Breath "—to mind their own bloody business."

"Yes, sir. Thank you for your time."

He made his way down the stairs and to his car.

Jim turned his attention to us. "Dying has some—" Breath "—advantages."

"That's not funny, Dad."

I laughed. Cunning old man. "That poor man had no idea what to do. He didn't even ask to look around."

Emily sat back down in her chair. "He wouldn't have found anything anyway. We took everything with Shorty."

Jim's eyes lit up. "Show Luke."

Emily pulled out her phone and pulled up her messages. Shorty's little brown face stared up at me, as did a white one.

"The family who took Shorty didn't want him to be lonely. They got him a little brother to keep him company."

"Oh, that's sweet." I kept scrolling. There was rabbit hutch that would rival the Taj Mahal.

"That's their home for a couple of hours every day. The rest of the time they live inside and rule the house."

Jim smiled and gripped at the arms of his chair.

"Are you ready for a sleep?" Emily asked him.

He nodded. Emily helped him out of his chair and into the wheelchair. He was so light she didn't need my help. I watched her wheel him away. My heart dropped every time she did, fearing it would be the last time I'd see him.

"Let's go over to St Clair to do some shopping," Emily said as she came out the door. "Then I'd like to drop into the co-op meeting to have a few words."

CHAPTER TWENTY-SEVEN

Emily

"ARE you sure you want to do this?" Luke asked as we sat in the car, outside the meeting hall, staring at the door.

"Yes." I wasn't sure what I was going to say to them, but I had to say something. Calling the department on my dad was a low act.

Luke opened his door. "Let's go then."

We walked to the building hand in hand. When we stepped inside, I broke into a sweat like I'd just stepped into a sauna. Luke guided me to some seats at the back. Ironic that they were our old seats. The noise in the room disappeared. The sweat warm on my skin moments ago chilled me. When I dared to look around, everyone was staring. I closed my eyes. I needed to realign myself with the determined person I seemed to have left back in the car. Opening my eyes again, I nodded to myself.

The room was just like it had always been. The walls were plain except for the photos of co-op presidents, past and present. Funny how the old presidents who'd served over multiple years only had one photo with the years noted below that, but Mrs Phillips had a photo for every year she'd served. She hadn't aged in any of them. The other people in the room had aged though—grey hair, drawn faces, wrinkles, extra weight.

I met the eyes of every person in the room as they turned to look at us. Bianca's scowl warned me that a tirade was imminent. I was ready. Her hands went to her hips. "Excuse me, this is a meeting for farmers."

"Last time I checked, we were farmers," Luke replied.

"I mean real farmers. We don't want the likes of her here."

I sat up tall. "Well, it's unfortunate for you that I am here then."

Bianca glared at me.

"Why don't you continue with your meeting? Or is it too *awks* for you to talk about me while I'm here."

Bianca stamped her foot and turned to her mother.

"Emily, you're not welcome here," Mrs Phillips said.

"I've never been welcome, have I? Not at this meeting. Not in this town."

Mrs Phillips pursed her lips.

"But you know what? I'm a big girl. I can recognise bigots for what they are."

I considered them all, making eye contact with the ones who looked at me directly. I wanted them all to know I was speaking about every single one of them.

"But what I don't accept is when those bigots target my father." My voice rose but it didn't shake. "Does it make you feel good to have a dying man investigated?"

Some people turned in their chairs and bowed their heads.

"Does it?"

"Emily, I don't know what you're talking about," Mrs Phillips said.

Good tactic but I wasn't having it.

"Eleanor, only a weak person would lie about their actions."

I stared her down and watched as she shuffled from foot to foot.

"We reported you not your dad. Rabbits are illegal," Bianca blurted.

"Yet, no rabbit was found."

Bianca turned her wide eyes to her mother.

I stood up. "For seventeen years, I have endured bullying and harassment from all of you." I made sure my voice was loud and clear. "I have no idea why you would target an eight-year-old child who had just lost her mother. Did it make you feel strong?"

Bianca stared at me like the words didn't compute. I wasn't surprised. Anyone would think she was as thick as a blue tongue's girth, but her craftiness showed otherwise.

"The thing is, Bianca, I'm a successful businessperson. I don't need my parents to support me. I have friends who like me, not because they are scared of me, but because I'm a good person."

Bianca stood open mouthed. She raised her hands as if ready to protest. I didn't give her the chance.

"And above all, I have Luke. You will never have any of those things."

I glanced around the room. Some farmers stared blankly.

Others mouths and faces twisted in distaste. Others sat stiff, their faces like stone.

Bianca opened her mouth. "I have—"

"If any of you come near my father or our farm, I will report you to the police."

I stepped into the aisle and waited for Luke. When he joined me, he took hold of my hand and we walked out together. As we neared the car Luke pulled me into his arms.

"You were brilliant."

I smiled against his chest. "Thank you."

"How do you feel?" He pulled away and studied my face.

"Relieved. I'm happy I stood up to Bianca."

"The look on her face was the best. She had no comeback."

I couldn't wait to get home to tell Dad. I gave Luke a quick kiss and then separated from him. "Let's go."

SILENCE GREETED us as we walked into the house. My hand trembled as I ran it over my face. I approached Dad's room, my steps light. My fingers brushed the door, the painted surface cool on my fingertips. Holding my breath, I pushed the door open. I stood there watching Dad where he lay in bed. His chest rose and I breathed out in relief. Luke sighed behind me.

I stepped into the room. "Dad?"

His eyes moved below his lids.

"Dad?"

His eyes opened slowly. He smiled at Luke and I.

"Emmaline. Luke. Are you two married yet?"

His grin lifted my heart. I went over and helped him sit up, arranging his pillows behind him.

"Are you saying you would give your blessing if I asked Emily to marry me?" Luke asked.

My stomach lurched.

Dad looked at him like he was dense. "What took you so long?"

"Well, you know, the fact she left and made a life without me was a bit of a deterrent."

"No excuse."

"I think it worked out in the end."

I narrowed my eyes at them. "Hello, I'm here too, you know."

Dad patted the bed beside him. I sat and took his hand. "Emily, will you marry Luke?"

I looked at Luke. He stared right back at me. My stomach tightened in anticipation. "Don't you think he should be the one to ask?"

CHAPTER TWENTY-EIGHT

Luke

JIM WATCHED my every move as I approached Emily. Talk about making a guy nervous. I didn't even know why I was nervous. I'd wanted this for forever. I'd wanted Emily forever. Dropping down onto one knee, I took Emily's hand.

"Emily, will you marry me?"

She watched my lips as they said the words but didn't respond. Instead, she bit her lip. What the hell?

One second. Two seconds.

She launched herself at me and wrapped her arms around my neck. Before uttering a word, she kissed me and hugged me and kissed me again. "Yes. A million times, yes."

"About bloody time," Jim said, his voice strained.

Emily returned to her father's side and took his hand. I pulled up a chair beside them.

"Emily has something else to tell you."

She blushed. "We went to the farmers co-op meeting tonight."

Jim stiffened. "And?"

"And I told them all that they're bullies."

Jim looked at Emily. "Did you?"

"Yes, and I told them if they didn't leave us alone, I would report them."

"Well done."

"Best of all, she told Bianca that she was pathetic."

"I didn't say that."

"No, but that's what it all boiled down to."

Jim smiled. He patted Emily's hand. "I'm proud of you, Emily. You're free now."

Her face glowed.

For her to be free it would mean her not living here. Not in this house or mine and I wouldn't expect her to. That meant I needed to leave the only home I knew and my parents. What would happen to the farm? I was always expected to take it over.

"Why don't you go and tell Steve and Bernie?"

"Do you want something to eat before we go?"

"I'm not hungry. I'm feeling tired. I'll just go back to sleep."

Emily stood and kissed Jim on the forehead.

Jim beckoned me over. "Good job, son. It's all about the two of you now."

I nodded. Us. It was about us.

We walked through the field hand in hand. We'd walked this path many times as children and teenagers. Together or to each other. Sometimes we ran in eagerness if there was something we wanted to share. This time we were together to share our news with the second most important people in my life.

"What are you thinking?" Emily asked.

"About how many times we've walked this path."

"It feels different today," she said, looking up at me.

I nodded. Everything felt different. Even the earth under my feet. In this place I felt safe and secure. I'd known the land since I could crawl. The dirt was inground into the lines of my hands, into the soles of my feet. It was part of me. But as I walked along the path in that moment, it was like we were two separate beings. It wasn't the land I belonged with; it was Emily. The land I stood on was the surface, she was my core.

Emily tugged on my hand and I turned my attention to her.

"Are you nervous?" she asked.

I gave her a small smile. I couldn't hide anything from her. Except my love all those years. Maybe she couldn't see it because she was too busy hiding hers.

"I guess so. I know my parents will be happy for us, but I don't want to disappoint them."

She tilted her head, her eyebrows drawn together. "How would you disappoint them?"

Before I could explain, we'd arrived. Mum waved to us from the kitchen window. When we entered, Dad raised his eyes from the paper he was reading. "Nice of you to grace us with your presence."

"Did you take sarcasm lessons with Jim?" I asked.

Dad laughed, his eyes crinkling at the sides. "We both got As."

Mum shook her head as she dried her hands. "Those two were such trouble at school. I'm sure the teachers were relieved when they left."

I nodded. My heart beat fast. Everyone stared at me as I

took a deep breath. This was absurd. They were my parents. They'd understand.

"Emily and I have news."

Mum looked at us, her eyes wide. She shifted from foot to foot like a child waiting for a bag of lollies. "Well?"

"We're getting married."

"Oh, that's wonderful," Mum said, embracing us both.

"About bloody time." Dad got out of his chair. He hugged me and clapped me on the back, then he kissed Emily.

"Sit down," Mum said, pulling chairs out. "Tell us all about it. How did you ask?" She was so excited I felt guilty she hadn't been there to see it. She laughed as we told her the story and didn't seem upset at all.

"Have you set a date?"

Emily shook her head.

"The sooner the better so Jim can be there," Dad said.

"We hadn't thought that far ahead," Emily said. She turned to me. It was a no brainer, but she still asked me anyway. "Can we do it soon?"

I put my arm around her shoulders and pulled her close. "Of course."

Mum looked between us. "There's so much to do. We need to think about guests and food and the venue."

Emily reached over and took hold of Mum's hand settling her. She turned to me, "I don't want many guests. Do you?"

"No. Just our parents and Aisha and Dalir, and we don't need a fancy venue. I'd be happy just to have a meal at home."

"Me too."

Mum nodded.

"But you need a dress." Her voice was firm, and I doubt

neither of us would be able to dissuade her even if we wanted to.

"Yes, I'll need a dress," I said. "But nothing too short, my legs aren't pretty like Emily's."

Emily held her laughter in. Dad shook his head. Mum just ignored me.

"How long does it take to get married nowadays? You're going to need an official." Mum was typing into her phone. "Oh."

"Oh what?" I asked trying to look at the screen.

"You have to submit your notice of intent to marry a month before."

My shoulders dropped. I made sure I had a firm hold on Emily's hand.

"Surely, there's a way to do it sooner," Dad said.

"I'm checking." Mum typed quickly. "You can apply for an exemption due to medical reasons in Victoria. It says the thirty days can be reduced to three. I'm trying to see if you can do the same in Queensland."

Silence filled the room as we waited. I did my best to keep calm. The thought of Jim missing the wedding brought tears to my eyes. After all these years, Emily and Jim were finally reconciled, and it would be unfair for them not to be together on our wedding day.

"There's an exemption here too. We need to get a letter from Jim's doctor, fill in some forms, and find a celebrant."

Emily turned to me. Her unshed tears mirrored mine. I hugged her close, kissing her head. "It's OK. We can get it done in time."

"I'll print out the forms," Mum said. "Tomorrow we can start ringing celebrants."

"I'll call Dr Hans in the morning to get a letter," Emily said.

"And once that's all sorted, we can find a dress and rings." Mum stood up and hugged Emily's shoulders.

"There's one more thing we need to talk about." My insides shook like they had been taken over by an earth tremor.

Mum and Dad turned to me. At that moment I realised I hadn't spoken to Emily about it. Shit. I hoped she'd understand. Not a great way to start our life together, making decisions without her.

I leant over and spoke to Emily, my voice low. "Sorry I didn't speak to you about this first." I turned back to my parents. I couldn't look at them. I couldn't. I had to. I was certain of my future and they needed to know. "Emily and I will live with Jim until he passes. After that, we'll be moving away."

Emily tilted her head, questioning me silently. I gave her a small smile. She held my hand tighter, and I loved her more in that moment. She knew how hard this was for me, but she didn't question me in front of my parents. She didn't allow me to doubt myself.

"Moving where?" Dad asked.

"I don't know yet. We haven't discussed it, but I can't expect Emily to live here, in this town."

"What about the farm?" Mum asked, putting down her phone.

"I'm sorry. I don't want to disappoint you."

I wanted them to say that they loved me and supported me no matter what. "I know the plan was for me to take over the farm. I know that's what we've all been working towards. I can't go ahead with that now."

The thumping of my heart echoed in my head as I watched my parents' unreadable faces. I imagined Emily's strength transferring from her to me through our joined hands. If I had Emily everything would be alright. Would they understand that Emily meant everything to me?

CHAPTER TWENTY-NINE

Emily

I COULDN'T PROCESS what he was doing. Luke never wanted to let anyone down. He wanted to please people to the detriment of himself. This, what he was doing now, was brave. This would be destroying him on the inside. The farm was his family legacy. My heart expanded knowing he was doing it for me. I held Luke's hand tight. Sometimes bravery needed reassurance.

I don't know where I was expecting to live. I hadn't thought of anything beyond saying yes to marrying Luke. And even before that I'd had so much on my mind with Dad, the farm, and my business, being with Luke was my relief every day. I didn't think much beyond that. Would I have moved back for him? Now that I'd faced them all, I could have. For him, I would have.

He never would have considered it fifteen years ago. He hadn't been strong enough seven years ago. I never thought it was something he'd ever do.

"You want us to sell?" Steve asked, his voice even. Is that what Luke wanted?

"I want you to do what's right for you. If you want to stay, I can help as much as I can. It just won't be full time. If you want to sell, I can help you get the farm ready."

Steve and Bernie looked at each other across the table. Steve considered us and then spoke. "I'm not going to say this surprises me. I've been expecting it since the two of you were twelve. When Emily returned and offered you a position in her business, it was pretty much all written on the wall."

Luke glanced at me and I knew what he was thinking— everyone knew we were destined to be together, except us.

Bernie nodded. "When you didn't follow Emily when she went to uni, we were shocked."

Luke shrugged. "Emily didn't want me. She had a whole new life to live. My life was here."

"I did want you."

Luke stared at me.

Bernie and Steve laughed and laughed. Steve spoke, breathless. "Luke, they say men are pretty dumb but you son..."

"Maybe the two of you could have helped," Luke pointed out.

"Only you two could have figured it out."

Luke stood up, a bewildered smile on his face. "I'm going to walk Emily home," he said before going to his mum and giving her a kiss.

She patted his face. "We're not disappointed, Luke. We're very happy."

As soon as we cleared the light from the house, I stopped.

"Are you sure this is what you want to do? If you don't want to—"

"I'm sure. I want to start a life together building on our dreams. It won't work for us here."

I wrapped my arms around Luke's neck. "I love you."

He bent his head to kiss me. As he grabbed my butt and lifted me, heat spread through me. His hardness pressed into me. Our kiss deepened until Luke pulled his lips away. "Let's go for a swim."

"What?"

"Over the road. In Jonesy's dam."

I looked in the direction of the dam. The darkness that enveloped us prevented me from even seeing the road.

"Like we used to do."

He didn't need to remind me. The first time I saw the nearly naked Luke for the god he was we were fifteen swimming at the dam.

WE RAN to the dam in the dark trying to stay quiet in our excitement. It was a full moon and the light glinted off Luke's blond hair. When we got to the dam, I stripped off quickly to my bra and undies and ran into the water. I turned and watched Luke. He wasn't even undressed yet. He pulled off his shirt, his chest revealed inch by inch. My stomach tightened in a way I'd never felt before. I couldn't take my eyes off him as he bent down to pull his shorts off. The moon highlighted his contoured muscles. When he turned to me it was obvious I'd been staring. I blushed, and, thankful he couldn't see the red rising on my face, turned and swam away. My skin hot, regardless of the cool water licking at it.

. . .

LUKE WATCHED AS I UNDRESSED. His intake of breath was sharp as I let my bra fall to the ground. I pushed my underwear down to my feet and stepped out. Tingles spread across my skin as Luke took all of me in.

"It's not fair when you're still dressed," I said.

He ignored me. Stalking towards me, he licked his lips. I imagined his tongue on my skin, stroking, licking. When he reached me, he stretched out his right hand. His fingers trailed down my neck to my breast. He cupped it, his thumb rolling across my nipple. My core tightened. His hand let go and made its way down my stomach, sending waves of desire through me. He groaned when his fingers reached the warmth between my legs.

He shoved his knee between my legs and pried them open. My feet shifted, the clay beneath them was rough. He slid his finger to my opening and sunk his finger in again and again, exploring my wetness. I took hold of Luke's shoulders as my legs lost their ability to hold me up. Luke wrapped his other arm around my back to keep me from falling. His hair brushed against my face. I breathed his earthiness in deep. It would always turn me on. Everything about Luke turned me on.

Two fingers entered me. I adjusted my hips so his fingers could go in deeper. My legs shook as Luke slid his fingers in and out and found the magic spot, rubbing it rhythmically. In. Out. Hitting the spot every time. I groaned. The pressure inside me built. Luke rested his head next to mine and his quick breath warmed my neck. I moved my hips and sunk further onto his hand. Luke groaned in response. "Fuck, Emily."

I loved that this was turning him on as much as it was

driving me towards orgasm. Each time he groaned it drove me closer.

His palm rubbed against my hard, swollen nub as his fingers slid in and out. He pulled them out and rubbed between my folds. His fingers slid easily in the wetness. He plunged them in again, rough, and fast. My toes clenched. My legs clenched. My whole body clenched. I threw my head back and cried out as I pulsated around his fingers. He kept them still and found my nub with his thumb. He moved it slowly sending another tremor through me. I gripped his shoulders. Moaning, I came like never before.

We stood there like that, his fingers inside me, until my tremors subsided. He kissed me and then his tongue sought out mine. I loosened my hands. They made their way down to his shorts and undid his zip and button. I snuck my hand in and rubbed it along his length before pulling his shorts down. The brush of his shorts against his skin was audible in the still night as was the sound of them hitting the ground. His underwear was next. I guided them down his legs and helped him step out of the material pooling around his feet. The soft cotton of his t-shirt was warm in my fingers as I pulled it over his head. I rested my hand on his smooth chest.

CHAPTER THIRTY

Luke

Although it was a warm night, the air caressing my skin felt cool. I raised my hand to push my hair out of my face. The same hand that had been covered in Emily's juices only minutes before. The smell was intoxicating. I wanted to taste all of her—the sweetness of her mouth, the saltiness of the sweat covering her skin, the tanginess between her legs. I licked my lips.

Emily kissed me lightly. Her hand wrapped around my dick, gentle but firm. I had been hard before, but her touch made me rigid. My dick jerked and her hand tightened around it. Her lips kissed my neck. Her teeth nipped. Shivers took over my body and my dick jerked again. Emily stroked. Up. Down. The whole length. I bent my legs, bracing myself.

Emily pushed herself against my side. Her tongue traced the dip above my collarbone and then found my neck again. I groaned. Her hand stroked. Faster. Firmer.

She whispered in my ear. "I want to taste you."

Fuck. I could have come right there but her warmth leaving my side distracted me. Her mouth made its way down my chest, my stomach, licking, sucking. When she reached my dick, her tongue circled my head, before she took me in her mouth. My balls tightened. The warmth of her mouth surrounded me as her mouth sank further. I clenched my hands at my side as the pressure built. She stroked and sucked, taking the whole length of my dick. A guttural sound built in my throat and escaped. Emily's mouth left my dick. Her hand still stroked, and I thrusted into her hand. Her lips brushed my ear, her breath warm.

"You tasted good." Her voice was low and husky. I exploded in her hand. She kept pumping. Her saliva mixed with my cum as her hand stroked the whole length.

"Holy fuck." My voice shook as much as my legs. We stood there while my breathing slowed, and my legs stopped shaking.

Then Emily kissed me and walked to the water. "I thought we were going for a swim."

WE WERE LAUGHING when we entered the house. I tried to quieten down as Emily went to check on Jim. I was surprised to hear his voice, expecting him to be asleep.

"Where have you two been?"

"We went for a swim," Emily told him.

"Not in Jonesy's dam again?" A note of exasperation in his voice.

"What?"

"You don't know how many times that man called Luke's parents and me when you were teens."

"But we only swam at night time."

"We *know*."

I stood in the doorway watching as Jim looked up at Emily who took a small step back. Jim gave me the look and rolled his eyes. "That man has good ears. I hope you two behaved."

"Sure, we did," I said, as a blush rose on Emily's face.

Jim sighed. "I won't be answering the phone tomorrow."

Emily turned to me, her eyes wide. I imagined Jonesy calling my parents while she was there sorting wedding stuff. A chuckle escaped.

"I need to go to Luke's in the morning. Bernie is helping me with the wedding stuff."

"We need to fill in some forms and find a celebrant to help with an exemption," I explained.

"Otherwise, we'd have to wait a whole month." Emily sat next to Jim.

"No time for that," he said, looking between us.

"It's OK. Mum will find someone. We should be right to go in four days, five days tops."

"OK. Good."

CHAPTER THIRTY-ONE

Emily

"ARE YOU READY?" I asked Dad. I'd stayed in my bedroom while Luke had helped to shower and dress him. We were not risking any bad luck by seeing each other before the wedding. Dad was in slacks and a grey shirt which helped brighten his green eyes. Bernie had done the shopping for him. My dress was simple—a sand-wash satin slip dress, a low flowing neckline and a low back. It made me feel sexy.

"I sure am." He smiled up at me with a smile that lit up his whole face. I'd miss that smile. I tried to hold back my tears, but they slid down my cheek anyway.

"Don't cry. Not today."

I nodded, trying to stop.

"Today is one of my proudest days. Even prouder than watching you walk on stage at your university graduation."

The tears stopped as shock took over. "What? You were there?"

"I wouldn't have missed it for the world."

I blew air out, puffing up my cheeks. I wanted to slap him for all the time and love we'd wasted.

"Go fix your face so we can get out there."

I did as I was told, then pushed Dad down the ramp. Dalir met us at the bottom and shook Dad's hand, then he took the wheelchair from me. I took hold of Dad's hand and we made our way around the house.

"I love you, Emmaline. I couldn't ask for a better daughter."

"I love you too, Dad."

He raised my hand to his lips.

Luke was standing with the celebrant in front of Mum's rose bushes in full bloom. My stomach flipped at the sight of him in slacks and a shirt. Bernie wouldn't let him wear jeans. I tried not to laugh out loud at her indignant voice when she repelled the suggestion. She couldn't do anything to tame his messy blond hair though. And I was glad. He smiled just like he did every morning when he saw me, and it brightened my world.

When we reached them, Luke approached me first and kissed me. His lips soft, warm and eager.

"You're meant to wait until after the ceremony," Steve said, humour in his voice. Dalir and Aisha laughed with him. We continued kissing.

"He has at least ten years of kissing to make up for," Bernie said.

I broke away as Bernie elbowed her husband in the ribs.

"As long as it doesn't involve Jonesy's dam again, I'll be happy," Steve said.

Heat rose in my cheeks. That bloody dam. Luke shook Dad's hand. Dad gave him a small tug and Luke bent down.

They had a quiet conversation and when they finished Dad patted him on the shoulder. Luke's eyes were glistening when he turned to me. I couldn't resist kissing him again. A simple kiss conveying every ounce of love I had for him.

"Right, let's get these two married," Dad said. "Or the waiting will cause the death of me."

I rolled my eyes. He was lucid today and his speech clear; it had been touch-and-go for the past week.

The celebrant smiled at us.

"Emily and Luke—"

"Emmaline," Dad and I said in unison.

I COULDN'T BELIEVE I was married to my best friend. The only man I'd ever wanted to marry. I didn't want to let his hand go. I didn't want to let him go. We sat down together at the table; our chairs pulled close so we could be touching.

I glanced round the table at our friends, parents and my brothers and sister. I couldn't imagine being happier. They talked and laughed, filling the warm night air with love. The aroma of spices wafted from the curries Aisha had made. My mouth watered. Dad nodded eagerly when Aisha served him. My heart warmed when she gave him a small serve and asked if that was enough. She knew him well enough to know he wouldn't want to waste.

He picked up his spoon with a shaky hand.

"Do you want help, Dad?"

"I think I can manage. Besides, I wouldn't want to separate you from your Siamese twin."

Steve opened his mouth to say something but closed it

again when Bernie gave him the look. I thought she'd only reserved that for Luke and I growing up.

"I need to learn how to give you the look," I said to Luke.

"Kissing me will also have the same effect."

"Are you sure?"

"Test it."

I leant over and kissed him. Aware of where we were, I pulled away. Luke gave me a lopsided smile.

"Yeah, I guess that works," I said, turning my attention to my food. That man was too tempting for his own good.

We ate and talked and laughed until the air cooled around us. When I turned to Dad, his eyes were closed but he was still smiling. I stood up to grab his blanket. As I lay it across him, his eyes opened.

"Thank you."

"Do you want to go to bed?"

"And miss the wedding cake? No way."

"Time for cake, is it?" Bernie said, standing up. She went into the house and brought the cake out on a platter. "Woolies mud cake, just for you. Aisha and Dalir drove all the way to Toowoomba to get it."

Luke and I grinned at each other. The best school lunches were when Bernie packed Woolies mud cake for us. Luke pointed at the cake. No words of congratulations. No happy wedding day. Instead, written in white, was *About Bloody Time*.

Could it get any better?

EPILOGUE

Twelve Months Later

Emily

BERNIE HANDED me a box as we walked to the door.

"This is from your Dad. He asked us to give it to you when you settled into your new home with Luke."

"What is it?" I asked, as I took the box from her.

"He didn't say."

The box was the size of a shoe box. I took the lid off and handed it to Luke before peering inside. There were photos of me growing up. I picked one up. It was Luke and me on the night of our formal. Dad had written the date on the back and a short description. There were photos of my graduation, and Luke and me at our sports awards, amongst others. He had cut out articles from magazines where my work had been featured. Ribbons and small trophies from football and sports days at school.

I teared up. Dad had kept all these things for me. All that time growing up, I'd thought he didn't care. In the middle of it all was a letter.

"Let's sit on the verandah," Luke said, taking the box off me so all I had in my hands was the letter.

Bernie and Steve joined us. I read it to myself first. The writing was shaky.

DEAR EMMALINE,

I know that I wasn't the greatest father to you growing up. I loved you with all my heart and I hope that you know that now.

These last few months I've spent with you have been the best of my life. I hate thinking about how much time I wasted. I am happy knowing we grew closer together, more than I could have ever hoped for.

When I said you were the best daughter, I meant it. Not only that, you are a beautiful human. You care about the people around you and you always do your best.

The fact that you and Luke are happily married soothes my heart. I have never been so happy to see two people married. Remember our talk, partners will make mistakes. It's only natural. It's how you deal with them that will make you stronger. Be each other's beacon.

I miss you already and I haven't even left.

I love you.

Dad.

. . .

I COULDN'T BREATHE PROPERLY. I handed the letter to Luke who read it to his parents. Bernie and Steve held hands as Luke struggled to say the words.

I continued to look through the photos. Every single one of them made me smile. Most of them were with Luke. I studied our expressions, the adoration and love that everyone had seen but us. Seriously, how did we not *see* our love for each other? It made me laugh. Luke looked at me sideways.

I handed a few photos to Luke. "Look at the photos, at our faces."

He took them from me and sifted through them, smiling. "How obvious could we have been?"

"Blind more like it," Steve said.

I nodded and leaned over so I could kiss Luke.

"Jim warned us about this. He told us to make our house a kiss free zone."

"Not a problem. Emily and I need to go home, we have things to do."

"Does it involve kissing?" I asked, reading his thoughts.

"Lots of kissing."

"Off you go, then. Before your mother gets ideas."

"Gross," Luke said. He stood up and put the letter inside the box before closing it. He held his hand out to mine. "Let's go."

He didn't need to ask me twice. Kissing Luke led to other things and they were some of my favourite things to do.

"Good night," we called over our shoulders.

"Make sure you're working on making those grandbabies for us," Bernie called after us.

"Thank goodness we didn't build the house close to the dam," Steve called out as we walked across the yard.

It was a ten-minute walk to our house on our farm. I was surprised when Steve and Bernie suggested we sell both farms and buy a property in the Lockyer Valley. It was two hours from Alma and was a completely different world. We'd built two houses on the farm. Having Luke's parents with us was perfect. Steve and Luke loved working together and Bernie always helped out, just like she had on their farm. Because they were not tied to it, like they had been their own, they could do things they'd always wanted to do, like travel.

Our farm was our piece of paradise. We were working hard to turn it into a working sustainable property. It would also be a teaching place for people who wanted to learn sustainable farming practices. We were working on wildlife corridors, rehabilitating the land for both the flora and fauna. Luke's passion and mine combined.

I peered up at the sky before we reached our house. The stars shone bright, and our fields were bathed in moonlight.

Luke gave Dad's box a pat as he placed it on the kitchen table. He tiptoed over to the baby wombats and I followed. They were snuggled up in their manmade pouches, sleeping.

"They'll need to be fed soon," I said, checking they were warm enough. The heat packs still held enough heat.

"But not yet." He grinned and pulled me into the bedroom. "Time for making babies."

Hell yeah, anything with Luke between my legs was worth doing. I stripped off my clothes in record time.

"Eager much?"

He couldn't talk. He was naked already.

"Always eager for you."

His body rammed into me and pushed me onto the bed. We shuffled up together, so our legs weren't hanging off the end. As part of that motion, I opened my legs and he entered me. Holy shit, it felt good.

"What happened to foreplay?" I asked, between moans.

"Do you want me to stop?" he asked, a sly grin on his face.

"Uh...no."

"Didn't think so."

He resumed in full earnest. My hips moved with his as he thrust inside me. I held firmly to his shoulders so the thrust couldn't push me away. Forcing myself back onto him with every thrust intensified the heat burning inside me. My head knocked into the soft pillow above me, I wanted to shove it out of the way but that would mean letting go of Luke. And that was never going to happen.

His shoulders and back tensed more with each thrust. He groaned. The primal noise sent me closer to the edge. His dick hit the magical spot. I squeezed his shoulders tight. My back tried to arch but his weight held me down. I called out his name as I clenched around him. His thrusts were long and hard and every part of him above me tensed as he exploded. He thrust again and again, groaning as he emptied himself inside me.

We lay there, our sweat mingling, breathing returning to normal. When he rolled off me, we held hands and stared up at the ceiling together.

"I think we can add great sex to the perfect husband list, don't you think?" he said.

"It's been on there for a while now."

He nodded like he was pleased with himself.

"What happens when I'm pregnant? Does this stop?" I asked.

"Hell no."

"That's good, because that would mean we'd have to stop now."

"What?"

I reached over to my bedside table and pulled the tester out of my drawer. Luke glanced at it, then covered my lips with his.

THANK YOU for reading my novel.

The next book in the Love Down Under Series is A Bird in the Hand.

To receive a free short story, be notified of future releases, and to keep up to date with other news, please join my newsletter. https://www.subscribepage.com/p9p9yo

---

BOOK REVIEWS from awesome readers like you are the lifeblood of authors, especially new authors. Reviews help readers find new books and authors find new readers. They don't need to be long or detailed, even two sentence reviews add value.

It would be appreciated if you could leave a review here:

Amazon

Goodreads

BookBub

OTHER books available in the Love Down Under Series are:

<u>The Cat's Out of the Bag</u>

She's started a new life. He's escaping his. Can two tortured souls find a future together?

Evie's a survivor. After rebuilding herself and her life, she's feeling the one thing she never thought she would – happy.

Until Jesse...

When she meets Jesse while volunteering at a cat shelter, dark memories of her past return. She is stronger now and wants to trust him, but after all she's been through, is trust even possible?

Jesse's a self-made billionaire yearning to get away from his empty life and the money-hungry parasites who inhabit it.

The plan?

Go to sunny Australia, leaving his old life behind, to find himself. But instead of finding just himself, he finds Evie, who is everything anyone should aspire to be. Now, what he aspires to be, is hers.

But to be hers, he needs to tell her everything and putting his heart on the line is hard.

The quest to find a cat a forever home leads them to travel across the country together. Will they find the strength to confide in each other? Or will the close quarters drive them apart?

When she left him…

…Tara couldn't explain why.

After five years, did she still have feelings for Shepherd?

Her brother's passing hit Tara hard and it left a scar. That night, at the party, when she saw Shepherd high, Tara had no choice, it was over. It brought up too many painful memories and she wouldn't go through it again. The decision was simple.

She had to leave.

No goodbye.

For Shepherd, losing Tara broke his heart. Not knowing why she left, well that pain he addressed with drugs, alcohol, and meaningless relationships. After he hit rock bottom, he cleaned up and came up with a plan to get her back. Could it work?

It was his only shot.

Would a desperate ruse, with the best intentions, but costing a fortune, give him the chance to win her heart for good? Or would it ruin him?

Will she be brave enough to be loved?

Get Off Your High Horse

When two opposites collide will their differences ignite a spark?

Frankie and Sebastian live totally different lives. Lives that are entwined through polo, the sport of kings. How entangled will they become?

Australian farmgirl, Frankie, has no interest in high society or the rich, arrogant riders she has to deal with, especially Sebastian. Her heart may be softening to his kindness and love of horses, but her brain won't be convinced. She's looking forward to her summer break on the farm, away from him...

...until her parents invite Sebastian to stay.

Sebastian never felt comfortable in his role as the Crown Prince of Oleander. He'd rather spend his days working with horses, playing polo and being with Frankie, whose fiery spirit has set his heart aflame.

But pressure from his mother, the Queen, to return to his royal duties is mounting. Everything he desires is in danger of being ripped away.

Can Sebastian convince Frankie that his hopes and dreams aren't so different from hers, or is he destined to return to a life he doesn't want, alone?

<u>A Bird In The Hand</u>

She yearns for the past. He wants a better future. Can they learn to love the present together?

When thirty-something Makayla's long term boyfriend pulls the 'let's have a break' card she is left broken hearted. Her best friends seize the opportunity and book a bus tour up the west coast of Australia. They hope distance will give her perspective, but she can't see past what she's lost.

Tyson needs a break from work and relationships, if that's what you can call them. When his mates plan the trip of a lifetime he decides to tag along. He's sure it will get him out of his rut, and and in turn, help him set a course for his future.

No one is prepared for the planning mishap that finds Makayla and Tyson sharing a room together. Their personalities clash – she's always too serious and he just wants some lighthearted fun. Add a fouled mouthed cockatoo to the equation and the perfect trip is not so perfect. Or is it?

ACKNOWLEDGMENTS

Cover by Outlined With Love Designs
Edited by Salt & Sage Books
Proofread by Claerie Kavanagh
And thanks to my amazing beta readers

ABOUT THE AUTHOR

Cynthia is a project officer by day and a writer by night. She enjoys writing about places she visited with her daughter while they travelled around Australia. She says that travel and reading are the best educators. Still, to this day, they both enjoy travelling and reading. A love of animals sees them feature in her books, some have small parts, others larger.

Find her online: http://cynthiaterelst.com/

All of her social links can be found here, Linktree: https://linktr.ee/cynthiaterelst

Printed in Great Britain
by Amazon

77463855R00135